NO SURRENDER
SOLDIER

NO SURRENDER SOLDIER

CHRISTINE KOHLER

F+W Media, Inc.

Published by
Merit Press
an imprint of F+W Media, Inc.
10151 Carver Road, Suite 200
Blue Ash, OH 45242. U.S.A.
www.meritpressbooks.com

ISBN 10: 1-4405-6561-9
ISBN 13: 978-1-4405-6561-8
eISBN 10: 1-4405-6562-7
eISBN 13: 978-1-4405-6562-5

Printed in the United States of America.

10   9   8   7   6   5   4   3   2   1

This book is available at quantity discounts for bulk purchases.
For information, please call 1-800-289-0963.

Chamorro Terms of Address

The purpose of this glossary is to familiarize you with terms of address in the Chamorro culture. Chamorros are descendants of indigenous Pacific Islanders in the Marianas who inter-married with Spanish sailors. Their language is a mixture of Chamorro and Spanish. Since the United States acquired Guam as a result of the Spanish-American War in 1898, Guamanians—Chamorros included—speak English. Still, their terms of address are Chamorro.

nana (nan-a)—mother
nana bihu (nan-a bi-who)—grandmother
tata (ta-ta)—father
tatan bihu (ta-tan bi-who)—grandfather
tan (tan)—aunt
tihu (tee-who)—uncle

GUAM

WORLD WAR II, JULY 21, 1944

Planes swarmed over Guam in droves. For a moment Lance Corporal Isamu Seto thought he was home in Japan. He was washing his face in the Talofofo River when he heard buzzing sounds. He looked up into the overcast sky and thought locusts were coming to destroy crops in his village of Saori. He blinked and shook his head. *Aiee, angry locusts turn into bombers. Amerikans must be attacking.*

Seto threw his field hat on and snatched up his rifle. No time to worry about filling his canteen or fetching his knapsack. Besides, if things did not go well in battle, Seto knew what his superiors required of him. To die honorably, and go the way of the cherry blossoms. He looked at the bayonet on the end of his rifle and swallowed hard against what felt like a peach pit stuck in his throat. He had pledged to die in battle for Emperor Hiro Hito. But could he commit *hara-kiri* like a true samurai?

Pain throbbed in his head. He did not want to think of such things. He must join his comrades and go to the mountains to ward off the enemy. Seto jogged upstream to find the soldiers, who were drinking *sake*, squabbling over a can of salmon, and eating three-day-old rice. He ignored the rumbling of his stomach. No time to break his fast—he kept his eyes on the bombers overhead.

Ka-boom, ka-boom! Shells dropped in the distance. Fire exploded upward from the earth. Seto ducked as if the bombers aimed directly at him. The soldiers scattered. Seto felt responsible for his comrades since they were young and of lesser rank. He ran, calling for his men.

Private Yoshi Nakamura leapt up from the above-ground roots of an evil spirit tree. Private Michi Hayato crawled out from behind a rock. They joined Seto, climbed the cliff, and ran toward the mountain.

Once together, they hung back at the base of the mountain. They crouched behind scraggly brush and waited. Planes continued to swarm and drop bombs. *Ka-boom, ka-boom!* Shells exploded—closer, closer. Smoke and the smell of sulfur filled the air. Rifle loaded, eyes fixed high above the ridge, Seto trembled. He waited for the *Amerikans*.

The sun seared through the sky, hazy from bombs exploding. It sounded like thunder as tanks rumbled over the mountain crest. Closer, closer tanks roared. US Marines advanced. Plumes of dust, shellfire, and rifle blasts clouded the air. When it cleared, Seto saw in the distance fellow Japanese soldiers lay dead. Those who did not die by enemy gunfire spilled their guts onto the ground with their bayonets. Some Japanese soldiers unpinned grenades under their helmets, and bloody, headless bodies remained.

Seto retched. His gun was no match for tanks and marines. Their numbers were too great. And his fellow soldiers too quick to die. He spit out the bile taste in his mouth. Tanks rolled over the crest and down the mountain toward Seto and his men. They ran.

Down the mountain, over the cliff, under the waterfall, into the river, through the mosquito-infested jungle, they ran.

Too many Amerikans storming the island. Too many Japanese dead, pounded through Seto's head as sweat streamed out from under his helmet.

Once in the jungle the soldiers stopped to catch their breaths. Seto listened. Gunfire and bombs burst in the distance. The men looked to Seto for a decision.

He wiped his mouth. "We wait."

That steamy, bloody day in 1944 when Americans stormed the island of Guam, the moment had come. Seto's moment of decision. Should he charge back over the mountain and face the US Marines with his rifle and bayonet? Or should he be done with it? He would disembowel himself like a true samurai.

If he did neither, Seto knew he would shame his family name, bring shame to the emperor and Japan. His head throbbed at this moment of decision. Bile rose in his throat.

Privates Nakamura and Hayato asked again, "*What do we do? The Amerikans are near!*"

Seto listened to the *rat-a-tat-tat* of guns. He smelled gunpowder and the smoke of cannon shells exploding.

He trembled inside. Seto decided one thing and one thing only. "I vow never to surrender."

CHAPTER 1

CRAZY TATAN

GUAM, JANUARY 3, 1972

Before my grandfather, Tatan Bihu San Nicolas, lost his mind, he called me "Little Turtle." Ancient Chamorros believed our island was borne on the back of a turtle that settled down in the Mariana Trench. I wanted to believe that "Little Turtle" was my grandfather's way of saying I was steady, strong like the turtle. He would say the turtle that birthed Guam spit me out onto the beach. Then, in his tough-guy way, Tatan would say, "You no taste good," and laugh his fool head off.

Come to think of it, maybe Tatan was crazy before old age robbed his memory.

I've wished I was a turtle for real since my older brother, Samuel Christopher Chargalauf, went off to fight in Vietnam. I wish I could swim from our island of Guam across the Pacific Ocean to Southeast Asia and bring my brother back.

Sammy being gone is killing my mother. Nana's brown almond eyes are red-rimmed from crying herself to sleep every night. I know, I hear her through the bedroom wall, sobbing as if she has hiccups that won't stop. My father stands around looking like he's in pain most the time. Like someone has a knife twisted in his gut and he's too stunned to pull it out. Seeing my family falling apart is making me feel as lost as Sammy and as crazy as Tatan.

But, looking back, if I had to pick a day when my world unraveled, I'm not sure it would be when Sammy left for war, or when Tatan lost his mind.

No, as horrible as those days were—what I thought of as the worst days of my life—it got worse. It got so bad I didn't even know myself. Didn't know how mean and evil and rotten to the core I could be. How crazy I could get. Crazy enough to want to kill a man.

It all started like any other day at my family's tourist shop, Sammy's Quonset Hut, which is named after my brother. It isn't really a Quonset building, rather a regular storefront a block from Tumon beach, which is like Waikiki on Oahu where all the tourists stay. My parents were sad and mopey about Sammy being overseas. I admit, I was p.o.ed, too. Christmas break was nearly over. I'd told my buddy, Tomas Tanaka, I would meet him at the beach. But instead I was ramming a dull box cutter back and forth into cardboard. Before my father left with a deposit for the bank, he'd told me I couldn't go to the beach until the shelves were stocked.

"If I had the Swiss Army knife Tata gave Sammy, I could open these boxes as easy as slicing mangoes with a machete." I was sorry I said it the minute it came out of my mouth. It was a good thing my father wasn't back from the bank yet or else he would have chewed me out for saying such a thing.

Nana looked up from cleaning a display case. Hurt shone all over her moon-shaped face. "Your tata knew what he was doing. Sammy needs that knife more than you do."

Shoving plastic-wrapped seashells on a shelf, I cracked open the top of a wooden crate from the Philippines and choked back coughs. I don't know what that straw-like packing stuff's made of, but the smell always makes me cough and my nose run. I pulled it off and reached into the crate.

Nana let out a pitiful laugh as if she was trying too hard to cheer me up. "Pretty pathetic when we import these." It wasn't working. Like I said, I was p.o.ed.

I held up a coconut decorated like a goofy shrunken native head and grunted. "You talking about coconuts or empty heads?" I chucked my chin toward Tatan, hunched over the counter doing nothing. He used to be tall and thick like an Ifil tree. But it was as if overnight his trunk buckled and branches bent under an invisible weight. My grandfather's weathered walnut face rarely smiled anymore, his mood always sour.

I shook the coconut. "We would've had this shipment unpacked weeks ago if it weren't for him."

"Hold your tongue." Nana shook her finger at me. "At fifteen you know everyt'ing? You don't. I won't have you disrespect your tatan bihu."

Ding, ding, ding. The bell over the door signaled for us to stop, like at the end of a round in boxing. No fighting in front of customers; that was the rule. Put on a plastic smile faker than the plastic Kewpie dolls in hula skirts. Those were made in Taiwan. As if all islands in the Pacific are Hawaiian.

Two Japanese girls came in. Probably college students on winter break. The girls shuffled up and down the aisles, pawing over souvenirs.

I had better things to do than watch them. I needed to leave before I opened my mouth again about Tatan not helping. I couldn't stand to see Nana all doe-eyed and hurt. Couldn't stand when Tatan yelled at her like a five-year-old. Couldn't stand it worse when I added my two cents and then everyone was mad at me.

Best I stock the shelves fast, then I could go body surfing with Tomas. Maybe Daphne would be there, and I could work up the nerve to ask her to go swimming with me. That'd take my mind off everything. Maybe even go reef-walking farther down-coast to catch octopus and sea cucumbers for dinner. *Hmm*, my stomach growled just thinking about it. If I had that knife, I wouldn't have to wait for dinner. I could slice up the sea cucumbers and eat them raw.

Two cases to unload and I'd be on the beach. I was setting up thimbles and silver spoons with Guam's US territorial seal on the end of the handles when one of the Japanese teens asked, "Where is Sammy?" She giggled. They always do, girls, they giggle behind their hands as if they just made a private joke.

"What?" Tatan said from behind the counter.

From where I was crouched I saw the girl in a sky blue bathing suit digging out money from her change purse to pay for a *sarong*. The other Japanese girl in a black one-piece suit and a straw hat pointed to the sign over the counter, SAMMY'S QUONSET HUT. Personally, I always thought KIKO'S QUONSET HUT had a nicer ring to it. Sammy wasn't interested in running the store one day anyway.

"Where's Sammy?" She giggled again. Any other day and the giggling wouldn't have gotten on my nerves. Daphne and her girl-friends giggled all the time and it never bothered me. But maybe that's because I know how smart Daphne is, especially in science class. That's why it doesn't bug me when she giggles; Daphne's not a bubble-head. I must have been extra touchy. Or, maybe that's just an excuse for how lousy I felt about everything and everyone.

Nana stepped up to the counter and set down a bucket of vinegar water and crumpled newspapers that she'd been cleaning glass cases with. "Sammy's my son." Nana smiled, but so slight the dimple in her left cheek barely showed. "He's . . . " She took a breath, straightened her shoulders, and lifted her chin. "Sammy is a navigator for the US Air Force stationed in Vietnam."

Everyone knew that meant Sammy was flying missions over enemy territory on a daily basis. At least, I knew it. All I ever heard about was how proud my parents were of my big brother. Nana lived for the day when Sammy's four-year hitch would be up. He could get out of the military and come home for good. Maybe then there would be no more talk of war, or the fear of death hanging like a storm cloud over our family.

I knocked down the coconut heads like bowling pins. Shoot, I'd have to do double the work to set them up again.

The girl who asked about Sammy blushed and bowed her head toward Nana.

Nana didn't return the bow. She didn't so much as nod. She just stood as tall as her short body would stretch. But her smile widened and her dimple creased deep as a crater in her round cheek.

Nana moved out from behind the counter and toward the back stock room. She smelled like vinegar when she passed me.

The girl in the blue swimsuit held out money for the tie-dyed *sarong*. Tatan rang up the purchase.

Did he have to look up every price? And look how long it took Tatan. Maybe I should've been running the register and he should've been stocking shelves.

The cash register drawer finally popped open. The girl handed Tatan the money. He looked at it, slid it through his fingers into the drawer, and shut the register. She shifted from one foot to the other. She cleared her throat. "Change, please?"

Tatan glared at her. He opened the drawer and fumbled through the bills and change. He slammed a handful of money back into the drawer, spilled coins onto the floor, and roared, "Damn yen, can't tell one from another!"

I dropped a box of ceramic bells and bumped into two crystal clocks. One shattered on the concrete floor. I couldn't do anything right. All I could think about was how fast could I get out of there.

Nana scurried toward the counter and apologized to the Japanese girls, while bowing her head and shoulders repeatedly. "I am so sorry. *Dozo*. My apologies. *Dozo*." She gave the girl change. As soon as they left she gripped Tatan's shoulder. "Go to the Chamorro Café and buy us lunch." She took a ten-dollar bill out of the register and handed it to Tatan. "Please." Her doe eyes pleaded with him.

I busied myself sweeping up the broken glass. I better let Nana handle Tatan. After all, he was her father, and she'd always been his favorite. Tatan shoved the money in his pants pocket and stormed out of the shop.

After he left, I couldn't hold back. "Those weren't even yen, just regular American money."

"Doesn't matter. I told you Tatan has *lytico-bodig*. I explained how the dementia would make him act—how he'd start doing strange t'ings. Can't you be patient with him?"

I stared at Nana. Me be patient with him? He was the one exploding like a volcano.

"Go to the storeroom and finish opening those shipments from the Philippines. When you're done, you can dust, too."

"It's not fair. Tatan throws a fit and I get punished. I'll never get out of here."

Nana sighed, as if too tired to say more. She picked up the vinegar bucket and crumpled papers and began cleaning the glass cases again.

I went to the storeroom and opened crates filled with straw mats, beach bags, and T-shirts. After a while I got hungry, and bored. Where was Tatan with the food? Maybe he forgot his way back. I swooped a feather duster in airplane motions until someone opened the screen door. I whipped around, expecting to see Tatan holding a Styrofoam container with our lunch. The sun blazed behind the person and blocked out his features. Still, I could tell it wasn't Tatan because the man had a shorter, leaner figure, like Sammy's. It was like seeing a ghost, which really spooked me, thinking Sammy had just stepped through the back screen door. But then Tomas's voice said, "Hey, Kiko, you free to go to the beach?"

I tossed the duster on a shelf. Once outside I could see the guy was my best bud, Tomas, whose Japanese body is small and wiry like Sammy's. "How come you not working today?" I asked.

"Vacation's almost over, bro. Didn't t'ink I'd be working the ranch when I could be here with you checking out the chicks in bikinis," Tomas said. "Besides, I slopped our sows earlier. When you weren't around to play baseball I knew you were working and needed rescued."

"Rescued is right." I'd slopped our pig in the morn and then worked all day at the shop. "I'm wheezing from this dust. Let's go catch some rays, waves, and babes. If I stick around until Tatan comes back, my folks will have me babysitting him next."

We took off to Tumon beach. Tomas thrust his chin in the direction of two white women in string bikinis sunbathing on straw mats.

"Whoa." He flicked his wrist, making his hand shake as if playing a tambourine. "Lookie at those!"

The white women didn't interest me. I had a crush on Daphne DeLeon, a Chamorrita from school. But I hadn't told anyone yet, not even Tomas, and especially not Daphne.

"Better not look too hard," I said. "Probably military wives. And when those Uncle Sams catch you, they going to punch your nose until your eyes can't see no more." That wouldn't take much either, since Tomas's Japanese eyes disappear when he squints against the glare of the sun.

"Oh, but it'll be worth it." Tomas panted like a dog. "Tell me again what Tatan says about bikinis."

I rolled my eyes. Tatan said it so many times it was annoying.

"Come on. Once more." Tomas laughed.

"Kay-o. Kay-o. Tatan says . . . " I lowered my voice to imitate Tatan's baritone voice, "Why call bikini? Bikini an atoll in Micronesia."

Tomas joined me in making exploding bomb noises—*Kaboom! Kaboom!* We wouldn't have dared make these sounds in front of Tatan. He saw nothing funny about the US military testing hydrogen bombs, or any other explosives, on Bikini Atoll.

When Tomas quit laughing, I imitated Tatan again. "Those swimsuits disgraceful. Look more like four hankies tied together. For shame. Put clothes on those girls before the priest sees them."

Tomas laughed as if this were the first time he'd heard it. He laughed all the way to the shaved ice truck to buy us blue and cherry swirled cones.

I laughed too. Laughed so hard I ran to take a whiz in the ocean.

As I peed I dug my toes into the crushed coral on the bottom of the bay and looked beyond the reef where I snorkeled. I breathed in the salt air and watched fishermen cast their seine nets. I wished Sammy was there and we could go fishing for *manahac* again. That'd be the life. Sammy and me fishing for rabbit fish instead of him flying over Vietnam and me stuck stocking shelves.

While I was thinking about the last time Sammy and I went fishing, someone knocked me on my butt. I was pushing myself up out of the warm water when the man surfaced and screamed, "Yee-ooww!" Blood oozed out from under the Japanese man's hands where he held his thigh.

I rolled over and tried to ignore coral stabbing my knees. The guy was bleeding bad. Not good. Fresh blood draws sharks.

"I'll *banzai* you!" my tatan yelled from the beach.

I squinted against the sun, trying to see him. Rainbows of water droplets bounced off a machete blade Tatan was holding. He sliced it back and forth as he waded into the ocean. "*Banzai! Banzai!* Take that, you Jap!"

Sheesh. He's really gone loco this time.

I started wading toward the injured man, straining to see if he was badly hurt. Tomas got to him first, took off his shirt and handed it to the man to tie on his leg. Tomas gave me a thumbs-up, then formed his hands like a megaphone and hollered, "Get Tatan."

I was in waist-deep water so I couldn't run. "Tatan! Tatan!" I called.

He ignored me and plunged farther into the ocean after the Japanese man. "Aye, you Nip!" my tatan bihu shouted, slicing air and water with his machete. Tomas swam out farther, trying to get out of Tatan's way. I didn't blame him.

"Aiee, policeman! Policeman!" the Japanese man shouted in English as he tried to get around Tatan. "He crazy! Old man crazy!"

Officer Perez, who patrolled the beach, dropped his bicycle on the sidewalk and raced toward Tatan.

The Japanese man was finally able to get closer to shore. But Tatan kept blocking his way. It was lucky for him that Tatan is an old man, 'cause he was slogging in slow motion even in the shallow water.

I splashed toward him. "Tatan! Tatan, it's me, Kiko! Come with me before you get hurt."

The policeman waded into the water. When Officer Perez reached Tatan, he came up from behind my grandfather and drew his night stick.

"Don't hurt my tatan!"

"Looks like he's not the one getting hurt," Officer Perez said.

The Japanese man held his thigh and looked trapped. Tatan lunged toward him. The man ran backward into the water, turned and half crawled, half dog-paddled out toward the reef where Tomas was bobbing up and down.

I bet the man would have swam back to Japan if he could have.

"Mister San Nicolas, sir. Put the machete down, easy like." The officer bent his stocky body until his seat skimmed water, showing with his hands how he wanted the machete dropped.

Officer Perez stood in front of my grandfather and held out both arms. "Easy. Easy," he said, as if warning Tatan a poisonous crown-of-thorns starfish lurked near his feet. One misstep meant certain death.

"Don't hurt him," I pleaded. "He's got *lytico-bodig*. He's not dangerous. Just confused, that's all."

I inched closer to my grandfather. "Come on, Tatan. It's me, Kiko. Let's go. Let's get out of here."

Tatan's eyes darted from Officer Perez to me, then gazed toward the outer reef for the Japanese man floundering in the surf. Water lapped calmly around Tatan's legs and half-submerged machete. He stood dazed, but with a crazed look in his brown eyes.

"Come on, Tatan." I reached for his hand not holding the machete. A glint of fear and confusion flashed in his eyes. I'd never seen Tatan like that before.

Officer Perez reached for the machete's wooden handle.

Tatan tightened his grip and jutted his jaw. His eyes turned fiery. "No!" Tatan jerked his machete chest-high. "He violated Roselina. He raped my Rosie."

What? I froze. *My mother?*

Officer Perez pulled his gun out of his hip holster. "Put the machete down and step back, Mister San Nicolas."

"No!" I stepped between Tatan and Officer Perez. "Tatan," I begged. "Give me the machete. We'll go see Nana. You'll see, not'ing bad happened to her. Just give me the machete and it'll be all right."

Tatan blinked, confusion clouded his eyes again. I held out my hand for the machete. "I'll carry it, Tatan. It's a long way to Sammy's."

Tatan's chest deflated as his anger left him. He hung his head and handed me the machete.

"Can you keep him at your store while I get this other man to the hospital?" Officer Perez asked. "I'll be back to talk to your parents as soon as possible."

I nodded, took Tatan's hand, and walked him back to our tourist shop, as if leading a lost boy home. But my heart raced, worried about Nana. Was it true what Tatan said? Was my mother raped?

CHAPTER 2

NO SURRENDER SOLDIER

JANUARY 3, 1972

"If I was samurai, I would commit hara-kiri." The naked Japanese soldier fingered the hand grenade pin. He sighed, then put the grenade back on a bamboo shelf beside his only other grenade.

"Alas, I am not samurai. For if I am samurai I would not be talking to a rat."

The rat twitched its whiskers between steel cage bars as if it understood.

"I am not samurai. I am Isamu Seto, lance corporal of the Japanese Imperial Army. I am not even a good soldier. I have shamed the emperor. I did not die the way the cherry blossoms go. I was afraid. Afraid! Do you understand, Rat? Do you understand fear?"

Seto shook the tiny cage. The rat recoiled.

"Yes, hide. For tonight you die with honor, Rat. Tonight you die as my dinner to keep these old bones alive another day. These bones of Isamu Seto, who is not samurai, not soldier, but a frightened old tailor hiding in an underground cave."

Seto laughed a stiff laugh, as rusty as his unusable World War II rifle. His laughter sounded muffled in the hollow one-yard-tall by ten-feet-long tunnel. Seto had dug it with a cannon shell eight feet beneath a bamboo patch in Guam's jungle.

It had been twenty-eight years since he hid on Guam. For fifteen years Seto lived underground. The last eight years had been long, lonely years of solitude since Privates Nakamura and Hayato died in their cave nearby.

His laughter turned sour. *I liked it better when I lived above ground in my bamboo hut,* he thought. *Why did the natives have to build houses closer to the river?*

He sighed, then pounded his fist on the dirt ceiling and cursed the rat. *"I hate living underground like a rat! Fear drove me here!"*

Seto had feared he would be sent back to Japan, and could not face having shamed his emperor and family. Worse, he feared what the *Amerikans* would do to him if he had surrendered.

He knew Japan had lost the war. About one year after he hid, according to his calculation of the moon and constellations, fliers dropped like bombs from airplanes informing Seto and comrades the war had ended.

At first he did not believe his beloved country could suffer defeat. Even though the leaflets showed Japan's divine emperor meeting with General MacArthur, he thought, *it is a trick.*

Over and over he read the words:

> The war is over. The Japanese Army has surren-
> dered unconditionally and a meeting has taken
> place between the Supreme Commander, General
> MacArthur, and the Emperor of Japan. This is no
> deception and no trap. Japanese military personnel
> should assemble without anxiety or concern at the
> Reception Centre at Agana, on the west coast of
> Guam, where arrangements will be made to facili-
> tate their early return to Japan.

Deception and trap, indeed, Seto had thought at the time. *Ha!* Japan could not lose with its *kamikaze*—divine wind—Buddha's blessings, and the divine emperor himself ordering the war.

Time dragged on. Shellfire ceased. Bullet sniping silenced. Seto became disheartened; Japan must have lost the war.

Still, he did not turn himself in. He was afraid.

His commanding officer had warned troops repeatedly that the enemy would execute all prisoners of war.

His father had warned Seto, "'Tis better to not come home at all and die a hero than to come home in shame."

Thinking about it twenty-eight years later, Seto felt renewed shame for having hid on *Omiya Jima,* the emperor's name for Guam. He felt shame for not having gone honorably by way of the cherry blossoms.

"*Har. Har,*" Seto laughed. "*A tailor! Here I sit with not a stitch on. Har! Har! Oh, but, Rat . . .*" Seto wiggled the tip of his finger through bars to prod Rat. Rat lunged to bite his finger. Seto withdrew it in time.

"*I wove cloth from pago bark that would have made Mama-san proud. I learned well as a child watching Mama-san, a weaver. I learned well from Papa-san, a fine tailor. Did you see my clothes I wove and sewed, Rat? Did you see my clothes I wore when I fetched you after sundown?*"

Seto only wore his clothes when he sneaked up through the bamboo hatch after dark. *No sense wearing out my fine hand-woven clothes.*

Seto proudly showed Rat his suit of beaten hibiscus bark, as if Mister Rat were a potential customer in Seto's tailor shop. He had long gotten over how rough the burlap-like fiber rubbed against his skin.

"*See? My two pairs of trousers have belt loops and button-down fly. Notice how I have sewn adjustable hooks and buttons on pant legs so I may run swiftly through the jungle. Not that I run much these days, mind you. Yet do you see outside pockets on my shirts? Are not these button holes works of art? And, aiee, real plastic buttons I carved from a flashlight! I'm afraid you only saw me in everyday shorts and shirt when I came to fetch you. If you like, I could dress for dinner, just this once. You like?*"

Rat gnawed at steel slats.

Seto sank back on his haunches and folded his clothes neatly. Noticing a rip in the sleeve of his everyday shirt, he removed a brass needle from its bamboo case. He stripped a strand of rope thicker than his hair. By the light of a coconut oil lamp, he threaded a pago strand into the eye of a needle and mended his torn sleeve.

Life had become routine. When Seto first hid in the jungle, he scavenged Japanese and *Amerikan* mess kits, bullets, tin cans, scissors, spoons, a tea kettle—anything metal he could take from dead soldiers, and later an *Amerikan* dump site, to make tools.

After settling, he sewed by day, foraged for food in the evening, and slept at night.

The only thing that changed was what he scrounged for dinner. Some nights it was fish, sometimes shrimp or crab. On less successful hunting trips, Seto brought home frogs and snails.

Once he snared a deer. He gutted it with his butcher knife, then stuffed venison up his chimney in a bamboo basket to smoke slowly so it would last a good while. The chimney sat at the opposite end of Seto's cave from the hatch in which he emerged above ground. The chimney allowed him to cook.

Another time he trapped a wild boar. By the second day of eating it, Seto felt as if he had vomited his entrails out. That would have been no death of honor, to die in the jungle from eating pig. Seto vowed to the spirits of his dead ancestors not to eat swine again, even though he found a fat pig penned up beside a house built not far from the edge of the jungle.

Seto was grateful for plenty of breadfruit, coconuts, nuts, papayas, and mangoes, in season. If not for the fruit of the trees, he was sure he would have starved. Although, he never developed a liking for breadfruit, so bland when fresh and sour when fermented.

Most of all, having chosen his hiding place by a river saved him. The Talofofo tributary was the water of life to Seto.

Seto clipped with scissors the thread of his last stitch in his mending. Then he snipped his hair.

"You like, Mister Rat? Do I look handsome? Handsome enough for a wife?" Rat stopped chewing the bars, cocked his head, and scrunched his ears forward. He returned to gnawing at rusted slats. *"Hai, I never marry. My intended is probably someone else's wife, or dead. I am*

but an old man. An old, old man beyond my fifty-eight years. Too old to marry. I see myself in the river. I see how hunched my back has grown from stooping in this hovel. No woman would have me."

Seto pulled his shocks of black hair and chopped it short. He clipped the ends of his scraggly gray mustache and beard. Seto scooped up stray hairs and put them in a coconut shell. He wasted nothing.

He ignored the rumblings of his stomach beneath his protruding ribs. Seto learned early if he ate when he was hungry, then he would never have enough food. He waited for nightfall.

Mended and groomed, Seto dressed, then climbed his ladder of bamboo tied together with rope. He removed a bamboo covering and burrowed like a rat out of his hole in the ground. That first whiff of night air smacked Seto in the face and reminded him that he was alive. He took a deeper breath. If only he could clear the rattle from his chest caused by soot from the underground chamber.

Tonight I shall treat myself to a bath. Seto brushed off chunks of cut hair stuck to his oily neck and back.

Seto searched deep into the twilight, deep into the mango groves and tangantangan vines, deep into the thicket of reeds and pandanus trees. He listened. He dared not speak, not even to himself, once he stepped beyond his hidden home. Other than familiar mosquitoes buzzing, frogs croaking, and geckos chirping, he heard nothing alarming to send him scurrying back down his hole. He ventured to the river to bathe.

He usually checked shrimp traps first. Tonight he rested in knowing he had rat for dinner.

Besides, he itched.

Seto took off his clothes and laid them at the trunk of a tree, where they blended in. The water was a cool relief from the muggy air. He bathed like a crocodile dragging its belly near the bottom, eyes peering up cautiously, nostrils skimming above water. He rubbed his scaly hands roughly against his skin in place of washcloth and soap. He emerged from the water and dressed. His cave was so damp, drying off was a waste of time.

Seto checked his palm-woven shrimp traps. Nothing. He reached into a sack and pulled out grated coconut to refill the bait pouches that dangled below the traps.

Next he checked his snare. *If only I could catch me a dog. What a delicacy and reminder of home. Or, the unthinkable, to toss my snare over one of those well-fed cows in the pasture.* Seto shuddered. *Too dangerous. Houses too close to my cave.* He reminded himself to stay focused. *About a yard in, just about here . . . aiee, as I thought, nothing . . .*

A twig snapped. Seto squatted down amongst the roots and ferns. Dead leaves rustled. Seto could see no person or animal so he stared at the ground.

A brown tree snake slithered down the tree his snare was tied to and across the jungle floor. Brown tree snakes were the reason there were no birds for Seto to catch and eat. Seto and snakes competed for rats, too. He often thought it odd he saw no snakes on this island when first he made it his home.

The snake slithered over Seto's net and advanced toward his leg. *Thwak.* With one swift stroke of his knife Seto chopped the snake in half. Seto took no chances on being poisoned. He didn't take the snake to his den to eat.

Always the tailor, he noticed two holes in his net.

No wonder I do not catch anything. He cut down his net, and stuffed it in his sack.

Concerned he was taking too long, and causing too much noise, Seto plucked snails off a tree trunk. He tossed into his sack a few coconuts that had fallen to the ground, and a breadfruit he pulled from a tree.

Like a hunched-over peddler with a knapsack on his back, Seto carried his treasures home. He lifted his bamboo trap door, and lowered himself rung by rung down his ladder. At the bottom he removed his shorts and shirt, then crawled through the tunnel to the slightly enlarged cooking chamber.

"Hai, Mister Rat, see what I brought home for dinner? And you, my friend, shall be the main course."

Rat had gotten nowhere for all his gnawing at the steel trap. He scurried around with interest at the sound of Seto's voice again.

Seto rubbed two sticks together to ignite a rope wick in coconut oil on the stove. *"Fire was much easier when I still had a flashlight lens,"* he said more to himself than to Rat. It had been so long ago since he owned the lens that he couldn't remember when he lost it. All that lingered were memories of anger upon discovering it gone. Some days he wished to trade anger for this numbing fear.

He rubbed from top to bottom, top to bottom until the sticks finally ignited the wick. Content the oil would burn, Seto diced breadfruit to cook with snails in coconut milk.

He unlatched the trap door and pinched Rat behind its head with two fingers. He grabbed its tail with his other hand.

"Sorry, my friend. It is you or me."

Seto cut off Mister Rat's head, tail, and feet with a rusty butcher knife. He drained its warm blood into a coconut shell. He sliced its belly and peeled off its furry skin like shucking the shell of a craw-fish. Seto gutted Rat's belly to boil its innards in coconut milk. He fried the paltry meat in a skillet made by cutting his military canteen in half.

Then he sat on his pago-woven *tatami*, clicked his chopsticks whittled from branches, and ate.

"Mmm. I like rat liver best."

CHAPTER 3

SAMMY'S BASEBALL

JANUARY 4, 1972

Sitting at our kitchen table, I wolfed down an egg and chorizo tortilla and watched Nana scramble eggs with a fork. The air around her was hazy from sausage smoke. How come I never noticed the wild gray hairs in her wavy black hair? I patted down my own bushy hair. Otherwise, Nana didn't look any different—same round face, same dimple in the left cheek when she smiled, same brown almond eyes.

Tatan must've been wrong. That's my nana he was talking about. It had to have been the craziness in his head saying that bad thing happened to her. It couldn't have.

Nana caught me looking at her and smiled. Yep, dimple's still there. She smelled like sausage and plumeria. I shoved the last bit of breakfast in my mouth. Tata had already finished eating, but was still drinking black coffee and reading the newspaper.

"I need you do me a favor, eh?" Nana was wiping out the iron skillet with a paper towel.

I flicked my eyebrows.

"Stay home and keep an eye on Tatan." Nana set the skillet on the back burner of the gas stove.

"Why do I have to stay home? I didn't do anyt'ing." I slid my feet in my zoris, determined to go to Tumon with my parents. I was hoping I'd see Daphne there. She'd told me Friday night after Catechism that her nana was taking her shopping in Agana for school clothes, and then they'd have lunch at the Chamorro Café in Tumon. I was planning to get our lunch that afternoon and maybe run into her.

"Kiko, please." Nana twisted her wedding ring. It was a wonder after twenty-eight years being married she hadn't rubbed it smooth. "We been over this already. Officer Perez said Tatan can't go to Tumon beach no more. We're lucky that tourist didn't press charges."

"I don't know why he can't go. Nobody got killed."

"Kiko! Officer Perez said the man had to go to the hospital for stitches. It's costing us plenty mullah for the hospital bill."

"It was only a scratch."

Tata crumpled his newspaper. "Enough!" he bellowed. "That man could have been seriously hurt."

I shoved my hands into my jam pockets. "But it's the last day of vacation." The last day I'd get a chance to see Daphne alone. "We go to church tomorrow, then back to school Monday." It was as if by telling me that she was going to the café, Daphne wanted me to come talk to her. I can't do that at church or school. I get tongue-tied. If I don't go, she'll think I don't like her. She'll feel like a fool and not have anything to do with me.

"Kiko," Nana spoke in barely a whisper. "Please. We need you stay here and watch Tatan." I stared at her rubbing the rose on her ring. Tata had made the ring from a bent spoon he found in the rubble of the Governor's Palace after it got bombed during World War II. When she worried, Nana rubbed her ring like old women fingered rosaries during novenas. "And try not to argue with him."

Tata put his hand on my back. He didn't hug me anymore, so his hand felt warm, yet heavy. "Son, we're sorry. But we need you to be a man about this."

I shifted my shoulders away from his hand. That sounded too much like what Sammy had said to me the summer before he left for the air force. *Toughen up. Be a man.* Then Sammy would wrestle me down and tease me about my puny biceps. Well, they weren't puny any more. But the words sounded strange coming from my tata's mouth. He usually gave in to me, being the baby in the family.

My parents picked up their metal lunch boxes and left. I stared into space, feeling bummed out about the whole thing, wondering what I could do to salvage the end of Christmas break. It was certain I wouldn't be seeing Daphne until church.

Tata poked his head back in the house. "Remember, no going into the boonies. Keep Tatan out of there, too." My dog, Bobo, tried to nudge through the opening but Tata wouldn't let him in.

"And how am I supposed to do that? Eh? If he has a mind to—"

"Just do as I say," Tata interrupted. "Our neighbors lost two chickens and they're worried a straggler's living back there."

"A straggler . . . " I muttered. Stragglers are what we call Japanese soldiers who never surrendered after World War II. As far as I was concerned, my parents used fear of stragglers as an excuse, like some people use the boogeyman, when they didn't want me to go into the boonies. I shook my head. "No straggler would last that long."

Tata let go of the screen door and it slammed. "Don't argue with me. I'm late for work."

I kicked off my zoris, flinging them across the kitchen. One sandal landed on the counter. I didn't even bother to pick it up.

Through the screen door I watched my parents hurry to their rusted out 1961 Datsun. Tatan was already in the driver's seat.

"Ready to go?" Tatan asked. "Where's Kiko? We late."

Tata chucked his chin at Tatan. I knew that look, it meant, *He's your tata, Rosie, you handle him.*

"Tatan," Nana said, "you cannot go to work with us no more."

"*Humph.* Got lots to do at the shop. Who going to run the register?" Tatan did not budge from behind the steering wheel. "Kiko!" he shouted. "Get out here. We late!"

I pretended not to hear. Crazy old coot. Nana looked ready to cry. It was all his fault.

Tatan stomped back to the house. Bobo wagged his rump until his tail slapped from haunch to haunch.

With his foot, Tatan moved Bobo aside so he wouldn't go in the house, which was one of Nana's few strict rules ever since I broke out with flea bites a year after we moved. My parents had to fumigate the whole place and throw out my mattress to get rid of the fleas.

The screen door snapped shut on Bobo's nose. "Yip!" he cried.

"Hey, watch it!" I yelled. "Look what you've done now."

"Me? It's your fault we even here," Tatan said.

"My fault?"

"Yeah. If you weren't in trouble . . ."

"Me? Me! I didn't do not'ing."

"Yeah. You . . . trouble, you lazy boy."

"So, what'd I do? Huh? Name it!"

Tatan looked confused. "Don't know. Maybe 'cause your . . . your flip-flop's on the counter."

I scowled at my zori laying on the yellow-and-gray countertop. I didn't dare say, *That's not'ing compared to the charred marks and blistered paint from when you left the burner on. We had to eat Thanksgiving dinner at Tihu Gabe's.*

"But it had to be somet'ing real bad you done." Tatan glared. "Or else why Rosie say I got to babysit you?"

"Me? Babysit me? I'm the one stuck babysitting."

"You lie. Now you in bigger trouble. I tell Rosie when she get home you lie to me. Maybe she finally give you that whipping you deserve all these years. But, no, Rosie no whip you like she should. But you wait, tonight be different. You in big trouble now."

"Talk about trouble." I wasn't biting my tongue any longer. "It was you who chased a Japanese man with a machete. It's your fault I can't go to Tumon."

"What you talking about? I no chase Japanese with machete. I want to, during war. Especially after . . . after . . . But I no do it."

"Officer Perez arrested you. But then he say, 'Take the *manamko* home, but don't bring him back no more.'" I knew that would anger him, calling him "elderly."

"You lie! I go get machete and show you. No blood on it. You see."

I wasn't worried when Tatan went to fetch his machete. It was locked in the tool shed next to the pig pen and curing shed, where Tatan aged meat. My parents never locked up anything before this, not even the house. But on Tata's drive home from work last night, he stopped at Untalan's hardware store and bought padlocks for the sheds. "Probably lose the dadgum key," Tata had said.

My pet pig, Simon, started squealing, then stopped, so I peered out the window to look for Tatan. "He's acting more loco every day." Bobo was sniffing and Tatan was inspecting the base of our cinder block house, looking for his machete. "He probably doesn't remember two years ago the typhoon blew to smithereens that old tin house of ours where chickens ran underneath." I stomped my foot on the linoleum floor. "Yep, not'ing could flatten concrete and cinder blocks. Good t'ing we moved out here to this new house by the Talofofo River."

"Pilar! Pilar! Where's my machete?" Tatan called. "Come out here and help me find my machete. Pilar!"

"Now he's calling for Nana Bihu, and she's been dead four years." I sighed and slid to the floor. I missed my grandmother, Pilar San Nicolas. If she were alive, she'd take care of Tatan, and I wouldn't have to.

Simon started squealing again. I felt guilty about not having fed him yet, so I fished leftovers from the fridge, went outside and slopped my pig. When I came back in the house, Tatan was lying on his bed, staring at the ceiling. I decided to call Tomas to ask if he could come over and play baseball.

Baseball would take my mind off babysitting Tatan. After all, it wasn't fair. I not only wouldn't see Daphne, but I wouldn't be able to get seafood off the reef either. I planned on bringing home an octopus and sea cucumbers, and maybe even a baby squid, or some oysters to throw on the grill. I scowled at the burnt spot above the stove again. Nana wouldn't let Tatan or me touch the stove since the night of the fire. Of course, she didn't say the oil drum we grilled on out back was off limits.

Mmm, grilled seafood. I took a deep breath and tried to smell the ocean. Maybe if I imagined enough, I could taste fried squid and chopped sea cucumbers wrapped in seaweed on a bed of rice. Nope, it didn't work. I only tasted the egg and chorizo stuck in my teeth.

But as much as I would miss eating seafood, I'd miss Daphne more. All because of Tatan. It wasn't fair.

I went into the living room and stared at the phone. Maybe I should call Daphne and tell her I wouldn't be able to meet her at the Chamorro Café. I'd never called her before. I put my hand on the receiver. No, wait. Maybe I'd sound like a doofus. Like we'd made a date.

While I looked up her phone number I practiced what to say. Maybe, "I won't be at Tumon today. See, my tatan got arrested . . . " No, that didn't sound right either. Besides, I didn't want to explain what happened. Daphne's nana already looked cross-eyed at me every time I saw her. It wouldn't help me any if she knew my crazy tatan chased people with a machete.

"I won't be at Tumon today, I've got to . . . " To. To. What?

I picked up the receiver and dialed Daphne's number before I lost my nerve. I'd just tell her I wouldn't be at Tumon today and I'd see her Sunday. Nothing more.

The phone rang and rang and rang. Maybe she already left. I started to hang up when a voice said, "Hello?" I quickly put the receiver to my ear, knocking over a coffee cup Tatan must have left on the end-table.

"Hello? This is Missus DeLeon. Who is this?"

Missus DeLeon. The cross-eyed lion! My tongue felt like a slug shriveled in salt. I couldn't get a word out.

"Hello? Who is this? What do you want?" Missus DeLeon demanded on the other end of the phone line.

Panicked, I dropped the receiver in the cradle. Great. I probably sounded like some pervert heavy breathing over the phone. Worse, I couldn't admit to Daphne that I'd tried to call to tell her I wasn't going to be in Tumon.

I took off my T-shirt and mopped up the coffee from the carpet, then threw the T-shirt and coffee cup in the kitchen sink. I'd clean it up later.

I grabbed another T-shirt out of a laundry basket and called Tomas. He answered on the third ring.

"Howzit, Tomas? I'm home. Tatan's grounded, remember?"

"How could I forget? Man, he was one wicked dude yesterday."

"Yeah, well, now I'm stuck babysitting." I fell back onto the couch and snaked the black telephone cord around my arm. "Want to come over? We could play baseball."

"I guess. I'm not doing anyt'ing around here 'cept helping my nana with chores," Tomas said. "I ought to be able to weenie out of those. I'll be over in a minute with my bat."

"Kay-o. See you . . . And hurry, it's driving me nuts being here alone with Tatan."

I put on my gym shoes and waited.

Tomas's one minute dragged into one hour and eighteen minutes later when he showed up with his bat.

"What took so long?"

"I couldn't find my bat. Finally found it out back stuck in banyan roots." Tomas held up his wooden bat. "Maybe *taotaomonas* took it."

"That's not funny." I didn't like someone joking about ancestral spirits that live in banyan trees. The stories gave me the willies.

"You never know, maybe the spirits play baseball in the boonies." Tomas looked ready to launch into a ghost story. A shiver ran down my neck.

"Come on." I shook it off. "Time's a-wasting."

Tatan sat in a stupor on the front steps. Bobo lay panting beside him on the ground, licking salt from Tatan's dangling hand.

"Good Bobo." I scratched behind his ears. "Stay with Tatan." Bobo looked as if he was about to get up and follow me. "Stay." As soon as he settled back down, I scooted past them both. "Tatan, I'm going to play baseball with Tomas." Tatan didn't so much as blink.

I trotted out and joined Tomas at the edge of the cow pasture between our house and the boonies, which is a really dense jungle.

When Sammy played with us, he was the designated ball finder, especially if it went into the boonies. The other choice would be to map out a diamond farther into the cow pasture. That meant we would have to dodge cow patties, so Sammy said this was the best place.

Since Sammy was in Vietnam, Tomas and I figured we better be good hitters and fast runners. Neither one of us wanted to risk going into the boonies. Besides, we were down to only one baseball—the baseball Sammy had given me before he left.

"Hey, Kiko." Tomas was first up at bat. "Maybe you should change the name of 'Sammy's Quonset Hut' to 'Tatan's Coco-Nut Hut.'"

"Hey, Tomas." I gyrated on the mound and wound up as if for a wild pitch. "Watch what you say about my tatan while I'm the one t'rowing the ball."

Tomas planted his feet farther back from the bare spot in the dirt we called home plate.

I repositioned my feet on the bare pitcher's mound. I spit in the grass and wound up my right arm, rotating my shoulder backward. Then I brought the ball chest-high and hid it in my mitt. I stood steady with my right knee bent and my left heel lifted off the ground. This was a fancy pitch I'd been practicing to throw the batter off his game and get more spin and speed on the ball.

"Who you t'ink you are? Tom Seaver?" Tomas yelled.

Smart aleck. I'd show him. I thrust my left foot and my right arm forward simultaneously to hurl the ball past Tomas's bat.

"Strike one!" Tomas called in his umpire voice. "Not bad," he added. "Bet you can't do it again." Without Sammy, whoever batted had to double as umpire and catcher.

I did do it again. And again. Three strikes.

"How come you so hot today?" Tomas asked. "You're slaughtering me worse than a boonie pig at fiesta, bro! Let's quit and get lunch."

"My turn at bat." I wasn't anxious to go back home to Tatan.

"And he winds-up . . . " Tomas imitated a sportscaster.

"Just pitch, eh?" I cocked both arms back, bat ready to swing, chin near my left shoulder.

Tomas announced, "And it's a curve ball, a little low, outside, and it's a . . . and he slugs it high." I hit that sucker so far Tomas didn't even bother to chase it. "Fans, looks like it's out of the ballpark . . . Yes, yes, I can see it now! It's, it's . . . "

What a beautiful sight! I hit Sammy's ball so solid it arched into the sky like a rainbow. I tossed down the bat and trotted toward the outfield. The sun blinded me for a minute. When I looked for the ball again, it was gone. I ran the line the ball flew in and dashed into the weeds at the edge of the boonies. Dang. I didn't want to cross into the jungle after it. Even though I didn't see it come down, I had heard the ball break branches. I dragged my foot from side to side to mash down the brush. No ball.

How many times had Tata warned me not to go into the boonies alone? He said deep in the heart of the jungle lived wild boars, swarms of mosquitoes, bloodsucking leeches, poisonous brown tree snakes, Gila monsters, tree spirits, and murderous stragglers. One of those things would have put the fear of God in me. But together? *Gulp.*

Yet my only ball was in there. Sammy's ball. Why hadn't I asked Tata to buy me a new baseball so I could put Sammy's ball on my shelf and not use it? It was a big deal to Sammy when he gave me the ball and told me to hold on to it. "For when I come back and we play baseball again." I'd teased him and told him how I'd whip him by then. Why did I have to hit Sammy's ball into the boonies? I walked in a little ways farther to see if a ball had whizzed through there. Nothing.

The dense brush swallowed Tomas's voice, calling me from the clearing.

I looked around to get my bearings. It'd be easy to get lost. I knew better than to wander aimlessly in the jungle. When I was about nine, I'd gone alone into the boonies. Sammy never let me forget. "We nearly lost you!" Sammy would remind me. But I figured Sammy must have gotten a scolding from Nana for not keeping a better eye on me.

The deeper I tromped into the boonies, the thicker the underbrush got. I pushed palm fronds aside. A prickly vine snapped up and ripped my jams. "Oh bugger." I picked out a thorn and licked the blood off my thumb. I'd have to hide my shorts or else I'd have some explaining to do to Nana.

Deeper, deeper I trudged into the boonies. Deeper in than Tata allowed. But it was my only ball.

Don't lose it in the boonies, I could still hear Sammy say as if he were standing beside me. *Or I'll have to fly home just to find it for you.*

I wished he could fly home. Besides cheering Nana up, I wanted that knife. It was spooky in the jungle. I'd feel safer with a weapon. Better yet, I wish I had Tatan's machete.

I tore through tangled vines with my bare hands. I stepped up on a fallen trunk to look around. Not far into the boonies ran a tributary of the Talofofo River. Upstream and uphill from there flowed a high waterfall. From the log I spied the river, and something white gleaming from the bulrushes. "Kay-o, now we're talking." Tall grasses whipped my calves as I ran toward the bank. I bent down and picked up Sammy's baseball.

Wait.

"What the . . . ?" I lifted the soggy ball from the water's edge and backed up two steps to study what had kept the ball from rolling all the way in and sinking to the bottom of the river.

A footprint? A small, narrow footprint sunken in the red clay had cradled Sammy's ball. "Strange, wonder who would be fool enough to be back here in his bare feet?"

I turned around and ran, jumping best I could over the underbrush I'd just mashed down. I didn't want to meet whoever made that footprint. After one leap my heel crunched down on something slippery and the rubber sole of my worn gym shoe slid forward, as if I'd twisted my legs in a bad slide onto home base. I dropped the ball.

When I picked myself up I realized by the shell and goo on the bottom of my shoe I must have crunched down on one of those giant African snails, or whatever the slime balls are called. I leaned over to pick up Sammy's ball, but recoiled my hand. A brown tree snake lay by a bamboo thicket. It was dead—whacked in half. I let out a whistle, then slapped my hand across my mouth. Oh, not smart. What if the man was still around? Chicken skin rose on my arms until the hair stood on end. I looked around in all directions.

A footprint? A snake cut in two? No *taotaomona* did that.

I picked up my soggy baseball and ran the hell out of there.

CHAPTER 4

DESTROY EVIDENCE

JANUARY 4, 1972—LATE AFTERNOON

The muffled drone of bomber planes overhead startled Seto. For many years airplanes that looked like gray whales breaching the waves had been flying over his hiding place. He never grew used to the flying leviathans. They brought back memories of dogfights in the air, and Japanese kamikaze pilots crashing to fiery deaths. He never shook the nightmares.

Seto reached for the metal handle of his oil lamp. Coiled like a cobra about to strike sat a wick from rolled coconut fibers. He popped the wood stopper from a coconut shell container he made and poured coconut oil for fuel to cook his food.

"Careful, no spill." His finger touched the lamp well so he could feel not to overfill.

He rubbed a stick up and down, up and down, until friction ignited a spark and lit the wick.

Seto inched the oil lamp ahead of him as he crawled on hands and knees toward the other end of his tunnel to go to the latrine. He held his breath and pinched his nose before lifting the square wooden lid. He squatted over a hole in the ground he had dug to drain into the river. He wiped with leaves, closed the lid, then wondered what time of day it was.

"My stomach says it is time to eat. But then, it always says 'time to eat.'"

He inched to the bamboo ladder and looked up the shaft. Light filtered down through a bamboo mat concealing his underground cave. Seto blew out the oil light and duck-walked back toward the middle of the tunnel to retrieve his pants.

"I sneak a peek, just this once." Seto pulled on his pants and climbed the ladder. He pressed his face against bamboo slats like prison bars. The thin shafts of light blinded him. He squinted his eyes and turned his head back toward the bottom of the tunnel. *Light too bright*, he thought, but was afraid to speak near the top by the land where free men roamed.

Seto put his ear against the bamboo. *Chirp, chirp.*

Only transparent lizards with funny flat feet, too small to eat.

He closed his eyes, bracing them against the light, then lifted the bamboo hatch a tad. He opened his eyes to a flicker of brown. He peered around as far as his neck would bend, scoping for men like a periscope on a submarine. *I spy a doe!*

He scrambled down the bamboo ladder so fast he slipped on the bottom rungs and fell smack on his bony butt. *"Ooh,"* he cried, and rolled over and rubbed it. He crawled to the netted snare he had been mending.

Seto wound the net around his arm, pausing to examine the one hole he had not mended yet. *"Not big enough for a doe to slip through. It will do."* He grabbed the tail end of the snare and climbed back up the ladder.

At the top, Seto stopped. He slowly opened the hatch and peered around again. *No one.* He poked his wild shock of black hair through the opening. Sweat broke out on his brow and ran down his nose. He stepped down a rung. *I cannot do this. Not during day. What if I am seen?*

His stomach rumbled louder than a storm cloud rolling in from sea.

Just this once. For a doe, it is worth risking.

Seto mustered his courage, stepped up two rungs, and stuck not just his hair, but his head, neck, and shoulders through the hole. The bamboo mat draped his head like a helmet. He twisted his upper body around and scoped out the entire region. No one.

Just this once. Seto slithered out of his hole. *I will be quick.* He crept out of the bamboo patch in the direction of the river.

He reached the tree where he had cut down his snare. He hitched his net over his shoulder, hiked his feet up the trunk, and climbed.

Seto shimmied out onto a solid branch, tied the vine-rope around the limb, and began to drop the net to the ground.

Aiee, what is that down there? Ah, the snake I hacked in two. How could I have been so careless not to bury it?

Before climbing down he checked all ways. No sight of the doe. When he looked at the river he saw two prints in the red clay mud on the bank. One footprint, one shoeprint. He heard his father's voice in his head say *Stupid! You have been careless and stupid!* whenever Seto made a mistake on a customer's order.

He placed his bare feet on both sides of the tree and worked his way down—right, left, right, left—like a salamander. He dropped to the ground, hunched down on all fours, and looked around again. *I cannot be too cautious. I have already made two mistakes I must correct.*

Seto duck-walked through the brush until he reached the decaying snake. He dug a hole with his hands and a rock and buried the snake. He filled in the hole, smoothed it with his hand, and set the rock, like a monument, on top of the grave.

He half-crawled, half-slithered to the bank of the river. He couldn't afford to make another mistake by standing erect and risk being seen. *Good thing I am used to moving this way in my cave. Slowly, then quickly. Like karate. I will be as a frog who waits patiently for fly, then zaps it with his tongue.*

Seto reached the edge of a clearing. He was within meters of the bulrushes by the bank. He froze. *Too exposed. I will be too exposed. Aiee, how could I be so careless?*

He looked both ways, then in front and behind him. *No one.* He duck-walked to the bank, bent over, and patty-caked the cool mud with his hands until the prints were gone. He snapped off a cattail, brushed and rolled it over the clay, then dropped it into the river. He didn't wait to watch it drift downstream. Seto scurried like a shrew, back to his underground burrow.

CHAPTER 5

WAR NEVER ENDS

JANUARY 4, 1972—AFTERNOON

I burst out of the boonies, holding Sammy's drenched baseball in the air.

Tomas was waiting for me at the clearing. "It's over, folks!" Tomas called. "The game's called off on account of . . . waterlog!"

"Waterlog! More like," I tried to imitate Tomas's sportscaster voice, "Kiko Chargalauf won the game!"

"Have it your way. I'll give it to you," Tomas said. "Can we eat now, eh?"

"*Give* it to me? I earned that one fair and square. But, hey, did you do this on purpose to go eat?"

"Yeah, sure. I easy-tossed that ball, knowing you were a power hitter today and would knock it into tomorrow just so I can eat your nana's leftovers. 'Specially knowing she probably don't have none in the fridge on account of your tatan burning up the kitchen and near-ly getting arrested. Uh-huh," Tomas said. "Hey, maybe we should eat at my house instead, bro."

At the mention of Tatan, I knew I better get home. "Nah, it's my fridge or not'ing. I promised I'd watch Tatan, remember? Besides, they say I have to make sure he eats. They say plenty soon he may stop eating good."

"The *lytico-bodig* Tatan has, like, what is that, bro?" Tomas said. "I mean, I know *lytico-bodig* means 'fat and lazy,' but your tatan, well, he's not any fatter than most old Chamorro guys, and he don't seem lazy to me."

"Fat and lazy, that's dumb. I don't know why they call it that. Maybe he'll get fat and lazy later, like Bobo. Eh?"

"Not if he don't eat good," Tomas said.

"I guess it's like 'old timer's' disease."

"You mean Alzheimer's?" Tomas said.

"That's what I said, 'old timer's.'"

"Sure, whatever," Tomas said. "Let's go check on your tatan and eat."

While Tomas and I walked back to my house, we tossed the ball back and forth, lobbing it up to see who could toss it higher.

"See those B-52s flying overhead?" Tomas said. "I'm going to throw this ball so high it bounces off the wing of that middle plane."

"Yeah, right." I chucked my chin toward the plane.

Tomas snapped back his wrist and heaved the ball above his head. Following the ball as it descended, Tomas turned a half circle, backed up, and fell into a hole. *Thud!* The ball just missed his head.

"Ouch! I twisted my ankle," Tomas yelled.

"You all right, man?" I offered him a hand. "Hey, what's with the hole, eh?" I looked around our side yard. "And that hole. And there's another hole. What the . . . ?" I pointed the bat to at least a half dozen large pits of different depths. Some were ankle deep, others at least knee deep.

Tomas picked up the baseball and glove and hobbled out of the hole he had fallen into.

"Hey, bro, you're right. This is weird."

"Tatan!" I yelled.

Instead of answering me, he was singing:

"Oh Mr. Sam, Sam

My dear Uncle Sam

Won't you please come

Back to Guam?"

"Tatan!" I yelled again, this time looking down at my tatan bihu digging a deep hole.

"What are you doing?" Only Bobo stopped digging, looked up, and wagged his tail.

Tomas peered into the hole as he stood like a crane on one foot and babied the other ankle.

"You talk to him," I told Tomas. I didn't know if Tatan was ignoring me or what.

"Tatan?" Tomas said.

"Say somet'ing in Chamorro," I said to Tomas.

"What should I say? You know about as much Chamorro as I do," Tomas said.

"I don't know. I just know his brain's more in the past lately than the present." I hollered down to Tatan, "Hey, Tatan San Nicolas, *hafa adai*, hello."

He kept digging and singing,

" . . . lives in danger

. . . better come

kill . . . Japanese

Right here on Guam."

Tomas joined me in speaking Chamorro, "Tatan, *si yu'us ma'ase.*"

"What did you thank him for? He's digging up our yard. How am I going to explain this to my parents?"

"You said talk to him in Chamorro," Tomas said.

Dirt flew out of the hole. I'd never heard the song Tatan was singing: "Oh, Mr. Sam . . .

. . . please come back . . . "

Tomas tried to get Tatan's attention by saying a few Japanese greetings he probably remembered from his grandfather. "San Nicolas-san, *ohayo gozaimasu.* Good morning. *Konnichi wa?* Good afternoon?"

Tatan stopped singing. He stood at attention, then bowed deeply at the waist. "*Arigato.* I did good, no? I dug holes like you said. Very good holes, no?" Tatan asked Tomas.

"Very good holes," Tomas said.

I ordered, "Now get up here, Tatan."

"Yeah, come on up here," Tomas said. "Excellent holes."

Tatan began to climb out of the pit, then changed his mind and scooped his shovel back into the dirt. "Wait, I find somet'ing. I give it to you and you give my family food, no?" Tatan bent down and rapped his knuckles on a metal object. "You like what I find?" Bobo started digging faster around the object, as if it were a bone. But no bone sounded like metal.

I dropped like a cat into the hole to see what Tatan found.

"Holy sh . . . *Madre Maria*! It's a land mine!" My heart raced and pricklies jolted up the back of my neck.

"A mine!" Tomas's voice cracked. "Don't move! Don't anybody move!"

Tatan struck the metal with his shovel and it made a *ping* sound. Bobo dug furiously at the other side, kicking out dirt with his front paws.

"Bobo, stop it! Tatan, don't touch it!" No one would listen to me. Frantically, I jerked Bobo by the scruff of his neck. I felt bad when he yelped, but I had to get him out of there. Tatan took up where Bobo left off by digging around the mine with his bare hands.

"Tatan, stop!"

Tatan kept digging. I'd have pulled him up out of there, too, if I thought I could. But Tatan was too big for me to wrestle, and certainly not over a land mine. I wished Sammy were here, he'd know what to do. I shouted at Tomas. "Make him stop! He's going to blow us all sky high!"

"Tatan," Tomas said in a screechy voice. He cleared his throat and tried again, deeper, "San Nicolas-san. Good hole."

Tatan stopped digging around the mine and looked up at Tomas. Bobo stopped thrashing and watched Tatan, as if for directions. I stood very, very still—on the outside. My insides felt like a motor racing in high gear.

"San Nicolas-san, I want you to dig another hole," Tomas said.

"Another hole? Didn't I do good finding this for you? I get it out and trade it for food for my family. Please, more rice for my Pilar and Rosie." Tatan bent down to dig some more.

"No!" Tomas shouted. Tatan stopped dead. Tomas tried the low, calm voice of authority again. "I want . . . no, I command you dig a different hole, San Nicolas-san. Now. Then I will give you more food for your family." Tomas added in his own voice, "Lots more food."

Tatan climbed out of the hole with his shovel. I breathed deep, then scrambled up after him, still clutching the skin on Bobo's neck. My dog yanked against me, trying to get back down in the hole to dig up the mine.

As soon as Tomas marched Tatan behind the house, I ran into the house and called Big Navy, and said to send a bomb squad. The wall clock tick-tocked, tick-tocked as I tried to convince the operator I wasn't some teenage prankster. After I hung up I thought about how long it would take the navy guys to drive from Apra Harbor to Talofofo. *Tick-tock, tick-tock* . . . any time was too long with a land mine in our yard.

Man, would my parents be furious with me if they came home and found the yard blown to smithereens the first day they left me home to babysit Tatan. I looked out the kitchen window. Yard? On second thought, I wondered how far that bomb would blow. I would never see my parents or Sammy or Daphne again. My insides raced as if on jet fuel.

I reached for the phone again and dialed the Talofofo mayor's office. "Send a fire truck to Ferdinand Chargalauf's house right away. Hurry!"

After I couldn't think of anyone else to call, I locked Bobo in the bathroom with the toilet seat up in case he was thirsty from digging. I shook so bad I bent over and tried to slow down my breathing. I felt as if I'd just finished a marathon around the entire island. One more deep breath, then I dashed back out to check on Tatan and Tomas.

Tatan was digging a new hole.

"What's he doing?" I asked Tomas. "And don't get smart and say 'digging a hole.'"

Tomas pursed his lips together, unpuckered them, and said, "Not any old hole, he's digging us a foxhole."

I stared at the hole with the bomb, too scared to go near it. If I could get Tatan out of his foxhole, we'd run for it. Anywhere, even the boonies, seemed safer than our own home.

CHAPTER 6

SIRENS

JANUARY 4, 1972—DUSK

Drenched in sweat, Seto shivered at the bottom of his ladder. *Whose shoeprint was that? Had he seen the snake?*

Seto could tell it was dusk. Faint streaks of light filtering through the hatch had disappeared. His cave was not pitch-black yet—this was the time of day he arose to hunt food. But he was afraid. Even to check if he snared the doe.

Earlier he heard boys yelling in the distance. He couldn't make out all of the *Amerikan* words, although he understood some, like "water," from when he supervised the natives during the war. He didn't like when the natives pretended not to understand Japanese.

How could they not understand? We taught their children Japanese. We required they speak it. We made them subjects of Japan.

Seto quit shivering from fear, and instead shook with sadness as he thought about how Japan lost the war to the *Amerikans. Did Amerika rule Japan now? Did Japanese speak English instead?* He shuddered. He did not wish to think anymore.

The other word Seto understood was "baseball." Ah, yes, he too used to play baseball. It was a very enjoyable game to listen to on the radio and watch. Baseball, one good thing that came out of *Amerika.*

To play baseball, though, was not always such a pleasant experience. Seto rubbed his shoulder at the thought of his lost childhood dream. He had wanted to be a pitcher, like his hero Eiji Sawamura of the Yomiuri Giants in the Nippon Professional Baseball League.

Sawamura was a pitcher who struck out Babe Ruth and Lou Gehrig when they played against the Tokyo Giants.

Seto flexed his shoulder back then relaxed it. Pitching was a distant dream. One lost in the years when he played outfield for his school team. At home, Seto pitched against the tool shed. At school, coach sent him to left field to run after grounders, or balls hit too high and far for him to catch. Maybe if his father would have worked with him. But his father let it be known baseball was a silly game, and hope of playing professional ball a foolish dream. Seto would become a tailor, like his father. And that was that, his father said.

The last letter he received from his father, before Seto transferred to Guam, said Eiji had enlisted into the Imperial Navy. His father had held Eiji up as a national hero. His father wrote in his chicken-scrawled script from too many years of gripping a needle, "I am confident Eiji will never shame his country. A true hero would rather die for his emperor than return unvictorious, shaming his family name forever."

Seto touched his dead comrade's talisman, made with a thousand stitches, and whispered, "May the gods grant Eiji long life." Yet, he wondered, did Eiji make it home?

Seto stretched both arms in front of him, cupping his hands around an imaginary ball. There was no room in his cave to pull back his arms into a proper pitch. There was no freedom of movement for play. His arms dropped to his sides. Yearning burned in his chest to join the boys who played at the edge of the jungle by the cow pasture. Many a day he listened for their laughter and shouting as they played baseball.

But the boys had stopped shouting what must have been hours ago. And there he sat sweating in the dark, waiting for nightfall so he could see if he snared a doe. *My stomach will not let me sleep tonight.*

He pulled his knees to his chest and wrapped his arms around himself. *"Shh, shh, be still my body,"* he whispered. *"A little while and I can rise from this grave, then eat."* He breathed deep—as deep as he could stand to inhale the stench of his latrine and burnt coconut oil—and shuddered one last time, then stilled.

"I wait. It is all I can do. Wait."

Silence filled his cave.

Sirens wailed in the distance. Sirens! Loud, screaming sirens. One, two, three, all cacophonies at different pitches. Wailing, wailing, louder, closer, wailing like air raid sirens warning of bombs dropping.

Seto flattened his body to the ground and covered his head with his arms. His body shook and shook, until it convulsed uncontrollably.

But no bombs fell.

Have they come for me? Is this the end?

CHAPTER 7

BOMBS

JANUARY 4, 1972—DUSK

"Tata! Nana!" I'd never been so glad to see my parents. I ran toward them but a fireman grabbed me and held me back. A bunch of neighbors had already come over to our house to see what was going on. I stood between Tomas and Tihu Gabe, my tata's brother.

"Stand back!" the fire chief ordered my parents through a bullhorn.

A navy demolition team lifted a dull metal object from a huge hole in our yard. One navy man in a heavy space-looking suit yelled to the crowd, "We got it! She's unarmed now!"

The fire chief raised his bullhorn again. "Stay put! We need to sweep the area."

Two men hauled the land mine away in a lead bucket to a dark blue van with white lettering that read, "US Naval Magazine Bomb Disposal Team."

My tata paced back and forth. Nana wrung her hands and twisted her ring. I wished I could be over there with her. Not sure if it'd have made her worry any less, but I would have felt a whole lot better hanging with my parents. My nana was saying, "What's with all the holes in our yard? Are mines in all of them? What's he mean 'unarmed now'? We've got live World War II land mines in our yard?" Her voice rose higher and shriller with each question.

"Lord, I hope not," Tata put his arm around her shoulders. "Or we're moving."

Several navy men swept the entire yard with metal detectors.

"All clear," one finally yelled.

"All clear!" the fire chief bellowed through the bullhorn.

The chief nodded at me so I ran to my parents and called, "Tata! Nana!"

My nana hugged me and I wasn't even embarrassed. She felt warm and safe. Both my parents' questions spilled out, one on top of the other. "Are you all right?" "Where's Tatan?" "What happened?" "What's with all the holes?"

By this time Tomas and the neighbor men had joined us. Word had spread there was trouble at the Chargalauf's house. Neighbor women came over and set up makeshift tables to spread out their dinners for potluck.

My answers tumbled out, and Tomas filled in the gaps, "Tatan dug all these holes, see."

"Bobo helped," Tomas said.

"Tatan wouldn't stop," I said. "Even though I told him to."

"But he listened to me," Tomas said, "when I spoke Japanese."

Tomas's tata, Rudy Tanaka, asked, "What you say?"

"I don't remember. Just simple stuff," Tomas said. "But he paid attention. Whatever I said."

"Yeah," I said. "Like Tomas was a soldier."

Tomas stood at attention and saluted. Any other time I might have laughed. But I was still scared. What if that mine had gone off while Tatan was digging? What if there were more mines in our yard?

Tihu Gabe said, "Hey, Tatan San Nicolas thinks the Japanese are still occupying Guam like during the war."

"Yeah." Juan Cruz chugged his beer, then raised the bottle. "Yeah, that's it. The *lytico-bodig*'s put him back thirty years in forced labor. Remember? The men had to dig those holes for the Japanese, and build the airstrip."

"I remember. We all did it," my tihu said. "Even though we were just young bucks barely out of high school. How could we ever forget . . . all that bowing to the Japanese. Me? I never bow again."

Juan Cruz interrupted. "Young bucks is right, that's why we dug the tunnels, hauled the rocks . . . " Cruz kept pointing his beer bottle at the holes Tatan dug in our yard. "Hell, we dug a whole canyon for those Japs . . . Sorry, Tanaka, I didn't mean you."

Tomas scowled until his tata patted Cruz's shoulder. "No offense taken. My tata was one of the first beaten and locked up. Japanese t'ought he was a traitor to their Motherland the way he helped American G.I.s who hid."

"Stop!" Nana shouted. "Stop talking about when we were prisoners! Some of us don't want to remember! . . . Kiko, where's Tatan? I told you watch him!"

I'd forgotten about Tatan. And I'd forgotten my nana stood there listening. Was it true? Did something awful happen to Nana during the war? Could what Tatan told Officer Perez about Nana being raped be true? I'd never heard her and Tata talk about being prisoners before. I looked down at my feet so I didn't have to look her in the eye.

"In the house, Nana." Warmth crept up my neck and head. I was just glad it'd gotten too dark for the men to see my shamed face. "I locked Tatan in with Bobo."

"With Bobo," she muttered. "I told you not to let that flea-bitten boonie dog in the house." She ran to the house, not even stopping when some of the women called to her as she passed them.

Tata eyeballed the other men. "Best let sleeping dogs lie. No more talking about war, you hear? It's hard enough Sammy being away at war. It's giving her nightmares again."

"Yeah. Yeah," all the men agreed. Then someone said, "Let's eat!" so they headed over toward the tables. Cruz grabbed another beer. He offered it to Tata, but my father shook his head and went inside with Nana instead.

Neighbor women brought lots of food—fish, rice, beans, *pancit*, tortillas, and for dessert baked plantains, papayas, mangoes, and coconuts. That's what I like about Guam; people party for no reason.

Tomas nudged me with his elbow, pointed at Daphne shaking out a tablecloth, and giggled like a schoolgirl. "Remember when

Daphne played Mother Mary? Bet she got an eyeful, especially being the *Virgin* Mary."

I flushed even deeper thinking about how at Christmas when the *Las Posadas* procession visited my house in search of shelter for Mary and Joseph—Tatan had stripped naked, crawled out of the bathroom window, and ran past Daphne. How much had she seen?

"Get it?" he persisted. "*Virgin* Mary?" Tomas giggled again.

Daphne smoothed the tablecloth over an old door lying across two wooden saw-horses. She looked up, caught me watching her, and smiled. "You okay?" she called over to me.

I didn't know I could get any redder. Pretty soon I'd be a blinking Christmas light. I had it bad for her. But I didn't want anyone to know. Should I go over and talk to her?

Before I moved or said anything, Tomas was already hustling over to talk to Daphne. "Yeah, we're okay. You should have seen it . . ."

By the time I joined them Tomas was talking a mile a minute to Daphne about what happened, as if she hadn't already heard. I just stood there, trying not to stare at how beautiful Daphne was. She's like watching a doe at dusk. Her tan skin looks so smooth, and her lips are like pink hibiscus flowers in full blossom. If I forget myself and stare at her too long, she gets shy and her lashes brush her cheeks like moth wings.

"Won't be long until Confirmation, eh, Kiko?"

Startled at hearing her say my name, I said something pretty lame, "Yeah, not long at all. April be here plenty soon."

I jumped when a wet tongue slurped my leg. Daphne laughed. It was Bobo. "Good boy." I rubbed Bobo's head and scratched his ears. "Nana let you out, eh?" Bobo nuzzled my arm.

Tomas rubbed his hands together. "Let's eat. Defusing bombs makes me hungry," Tomas said as if he disarmed and removed the mine himself, and not the navy bomb squad. Yeah, right. Tomas tried to make himself look like the hero, and then he led Daphne to a picnic table to sit down beside him. Bobo crawled under the table.

Daphne looked as if she was about to ask me to sit down on the other side of her, but her nana sat beside her instead. I wasn't about to sit with the cross-eyed lion. I can imagine that conversation. *Aren't you the heavy-breather who called? Stay away from my Daphne, you pervert!* Then Missus DeLeon might kick me under the table for good measure.

While I stood there trying to decide what to do, someone handed me a plate heaped with food. But my stomach was still jittery. I picked at it, then took the leftovers down to Simon in the pig pen.

Thank goodness no one mentioned the holes for the rest of the night.

Until after the neighbors all went home. My parents must have thought Tatan and I were asleep.

Only I couldn't sleep. For the first time in my life my parents yelled at each other. I lay in the dark and listened to them through the bedroom walls.

"I don't think we can handle Tatan no more." Tata sounded worried.

"I don't want to talk about it. Tatan's going to be okay. Kiko will help. We can do it."

"Tatan is not okay. He's not going to be okay. He's only going to get worse."

"Don't say that! That's my tata you're talking about! He's got to get better. He's got to, you hear?" It wasn't like Nana to yell. She must have been really mad.

"We can't pretend anymore. Tatan does have *lytico-bodig*. It's getting worse. How can we take care of him and run the store, too? And Kiko . . . " I pressed my head to the wall when Tata said my name. "Kiko has to go to school. Roselina, listen to me, I t'ink maybe . . . maybe we should send Tatan to live with your brother on Oahu, or the other one in California. They got more money and better, you know, doctors and hospitals and places to help them with this . . . this dementia t'ing Tatan has."

"How can you say that? Send Tatan to California with Tony? His wife's *haole*! She'll make my brother put Tatan in a nursing home. I won't stand for it! We're family. Family doesn't lock away family." It sounded like drum beats. I bet Nana was pounding her fist against something.

"Nursing homes are better equipped. It's not prison. It's a hospital, with nurses and—"

"As for Joaquin on Oahu, his Hawaiian wife is kind enough, but . . . but, Honolulu is too crowded! He'll get lost and not be found."

"You're being unreasonable. Joaquin doesn't live in Honolulu. He lives leeward side. Joaquin and Leala were good to Sammy the two years he lived with them during graduate school."

"And look where that got our Sammy—in the military! He goes to graduate school to study engineering and he comes back enlisted in the air force," Nana said.

"That wasn't Joaquin and Leala's fault. Sammy made up his mind on his own."

"No matter," Nana insisted. "Oahu's not Guam. Tatan will be lost forever if he can't live, and die, on Guam."

"But what are we going to do? When Kiko goes to school?"

The yelling stopped. I strained to hear Nana's reply. I got out of bed and pressed my ear near the crack where my door doesn't meet the floor.

Nana was crying. I wanted to go hug her like I did when I was a little boy. Tell her Tatan would get better. Sammy would come home. That everything would be all right. Nothing bad would happen. Not now. Not ever.

It'd be a lie, though. A big fat lie. Just like how I'd been lied to my entire life, thinking nothing bad ever happened to Nana before.

CHAPTER 8

GHOSTS

JANUARY 5, 1972

Seto lay sealed in his cave, listening.

Leaves raining on bamboo slats sounded like bones clacking.

Woo. Woo. Wind whistled through bamboo like flutes.

Gong. Gong. One large bamboo shoot drummed against smaller, weaker ones.

Seto could not sleep.

Planes droned overhead, muffled by dirt packed on top of him. Buried alive. Burrowed in his sepulcher. Still, Seto did not need to be above ground, nor at the apex of the mountain behind his *Omiya Jima* cave, to know bombers overhead wore no Rising Sun.

Darkness shrouded Seto's hiding place. This burial mound he called home. No matter which way he turned, side to side, front to back, he could not rest upon his mat. It itched. He scratched.

Seto tried to sleep, but to no avail. It felt as if thousands upon thousands of lice and beetles, cockroaches and centipedes and all the insects earth bore scurried millions of legs across his corpse.

Cold drafts drifted down his vault's shaft.

"No! No! I invoke the spirits, leave me alone tonight!" Seto cried. *"Sleep, Sleep, I beg of you, bring me peace."*

He shut his eyes tight. He tried to conjure up images of his mother, who smelled of spring cherry blossoms. He tried to see her steadfast fingers working threads upon her loom. He tried to feel her silky hair, faint silver wisps fallen around her face. He comforted himself by remembering her faded plum kimono, missing its *obi* she had embroidered and given to him to cherish her by.

Yet, he could not summon his mother's spirit, try as he did.

For they were marching. Marching.

Seto clasped hands over his ears.

Not raining leaves, nor whistling wind, not gonging bamboo, nor droning airplanes—especially not the bombers—could drown out the sound of a thousand soldiers marching. Marching. Marching.

It was the Japanese Imperial Army. His platoon marched through his chasm as if it were their purgatory. Tormented spirits caught between heaven and hell.

Ghosts. Spirits. Specters.

It mattered not what name they be called, Seto feared the ghastly ghouls who haunted him by night. Soldiers dressed in battle gear with missing limbs and open wounds reached for him in anguish.

"Why do you come? Have I betrayed you?" Seto had screamed this out to them before.

Still, no answer. Except for the sound of leaves raining overhead.

The soldiers marched, marched, marched through Seto as if he were the shadow, and they, the host.

Except for headless *hara-kiri* soldiers who placed grenades under their helmets, all other soldiers wore expressions of suffering.

"Look, see what I offer." Seto sat up on his *tatami* and showed them a paper under a sack that he filled with coconut fibers for a pillow. *"See! See the letters! I have written your names. I shall return to the temple and ask Kannon for mercy!"*

Yet they took not his gift, nor slowed their pace. Except one. He turned to Seto, and gaped his mouth open. A voice squeezed out, *"You are the only one left."* Then, he turned and marched away with the rest.

Seto smoothed the memorial sheet and placed it back under his pillow.

"Enough. Kannon, goddess of mercy, let this appease the dead. And may you send me no more uninvited guests tonight."

But, alas, his greatest fear was that mercy was lost to the dead.

For man is destined once to die, and after that, face judgment. There seemed no rest, nor rebirth, for these tormented spirits.

Exhausted, Seto settled in bed.

He breathed deep. Tossed and turned. And tried once more to shut out the horrors of war.

He napped. But did he? Sleep and wake hazed into one. What mattered if a dream be day or night? His greatest nightmares haunted him awake. Seto prayed for deepest of sleep. So deep that neither phantom nor wraith appear. Deepest of sleep where no memory walks, but all is dark and empty of voice. Seto welcomed that sleep. Yet feared the sleep of souls so deep that there be no waking evermore.

It was to that sleep of death that Seto and two comrade stragglers hidden in the heart of darkness sent two unsuspecting Chamorros. These young men appeared again to judge Seto's hand in their deaths.

Woo. Woo. . . . Woo. Woo.

It is but Wind playing her flute, Seto thought. He stirred, then settled on his back.

Woo. Woo.

Seto gazed up at his bamboo earth ceiling. Coconut oil coated it black. Iridescent pearl traces of the natives appeared. Seto wiped his eyes, then focused again to see if the outlines were but bamboo joints.

Woo. Woo. Wind blew her bamboo flutes. *Woooo. Woooo.*

"Remember us?" the traces said. *"We checked our traps in Talofofo boonies."* Seto recognized familiar voices, though in life he gave them no chance to speak. *"And looked for betel nut,"* one disembodied spirit said.

Seto knew who they were, though he had seen them alive only once. The night he and his two companions murdered the young men because the stragglers feared they would be found.

Seto closed his eyes against tears and sweat that dimmed his focus. He pleaded with the wisps, *"I didn't know. I didn't know. Fear made me shoot."*

"What didn't you know?" asked the one who wanted betel nut.

"How young you were. Or that your knife was to cut shrimp trap line. Or . . . or . . ."

The younger one, in his teen alto voice, helped Seto remember, *"Or that your friends would cut our hands and feet, slice our guts, and leave us to rot?"*

Seto cried, *"Please, have mercy! Let me be! Have mercy on me!"*

Seto knew not what to offer them. He had no shrimp or betel nut. His gods had no power to restore life. Broken, Seto filled a coconut shell with milk and tossed it to the ceiling.

"Mercy is not ours to give." They departed up through bamboo and earth. All that remained was the smell of burnt oil and dripping milk.

Milk fell like gentle raindrops, but could not quench the fire Seto felt inside and out. Seto, drenched in sweat, lay down again.

He trembled with night terrors.

"Oh," he cried in anguish, *"what must I do to cleanse myself of this blood that I have shed by my hands? Hands made to be a tailor, not a butcher.*

"Oh, by the gods, if you grant me one wish, to return to Japan, I will offer sacrifice and prayers in pilgrimage to the mountain."

Yet he feared he would never leave this crypt alive.

When fitful turns died down, Seto slumped upon his belly like a brown tree snake stalking prey, then snuggled his head on a coarse sack and lay still upon his mat.

Gong. Gong.

"It is but bamboo banging against its brother."

Gong, gong.

Two spooks rose up through the *tatami* and seized Seto's feet and hands. He wrestled with his comrade stragglers who died of poison. Or was it suicide? Not twenty yards away, their bones were sealed in a necropolis they dug with their own hands.

"You've desecrated our graveyard and stolen from us all we had!" the ghost of Michi Hayato said.

Seto's body contorted with fear, as if shaken by seizures.

"Over there," he shouted and pointed to a neatly folded flag. White with a blood-red sun.

"And my talisman of a thousand stitches," the specter of Yoshi Nakamura accused.

"It did you no good! You were dead! I took it, hoping each stitch would keep me from harm." Seto's fear stoked his fever hotter.

"Please," Seto begged, *"leave me alone. What have I done to deserve your visits? Have I even once done something cowardly that turns you against me?"*

Demons laughed heartily. But Hayato and Nakamura gave no answer.

"I am your superior," Seto shouted louder, trying to summon a voice of authority. *"I order you to leave!"*

Louder and louder laughter grew. Not like laughter of children frolicking by a river. Not laughter of newlyweds under their first moon. But rather shrill, shrieking, high-pitched siren laughter of eerie wind howling through grottos.

"Here, take flag," Seto bargained. *"I wanted it to remind me of home. And thousand stitches, those stitches were sewn for good luck by your kinsman and friends. Take it! Take it!"*

The spooks trampled the flag and talisman, yet left no telltale rumples to show their presence. *"How about your gun?"* Hayato asked. *"Would you sacrifice your gun?"* Seto fetched the wooden butt and rusted barrel of his dormant soldier's gun. It too had seen a thousand deaths in China and on Guam. Seto traced the Chrysanthemum. *"It is for my emperor. When I return."*

Hayato and Nakamura laughed a haunting laugh. The demons laughed. *Gong. Gong.* Wind sounded the gong.

They departed.

Seto stretched up on all fours like a cat and arched his sore back. *"It must be the rat I ate,"* he mused.

Stretch. Reach. He doused his face in a little water he had boiled and saved for morning. Seto went to the toilet, then returned to his *tatami.*

"Let me start afresh. Never have I been visited by more than these. My fever's broke. The ghosts are gone. Now I shall slumber."

He smoothed the memorial paper under his pillow. Milk no longer dripped from his ceiling. He placed his comrade's talisman on top of Japan's flag, and cuddled his mother's *obi* against his heart.

He then lay down to sleep in peace.

Drifting in and out. Out and in. Sleep fell in dreams and fits.

He smelled cherry blossoms.

"Tsuru," he whispered his mother's name.

Cherry blossoms bloomed in Mount Mitake-san, where his mother prayed to conceive. The mountain granted her wish and gave her an only son.

Three airplanes from the east droned overhead. Bombers.

His mother's plum kimono transformed into a billowing purple mushroom filling the heavens, with fire at her feet.

Seto searched for his mother in the fog. He looked for her loom. Instead, barren cherry tree branches like gnarled bones fingered silkworm threads upon her web. He felt for her hair. Silver wisps fell beyond his grasp. He longed to taste ripened cherries. Pits lay strewn upon wasted ground as birds pecked rotted poisonous fruit.

Seto curled in a fetal ball and embraced his mother's *obi*. He had nothing to offer. She stained her *obi* with blood-pricked fingers. He soaked it with his tears.

CHAPTER 9

BATS

When Nana woke me Monday morning, Tatan slept so soundly his snoring could be heard throughout our six-room house.

For once I was anxious to go to school. Since I couldn't go to Tumon, and at home I'd be stuck babysitting Tatan, at least at school I'd get to see my friends.

I scooped rice fried with scrambled eggs into a tortilla, rolled it, then shoved it in my mouth. Bobo whined and scratched at the kitchen door, wanting to be let in. I headed to my bedroom to grab a notebook and pens.

"Why in such a hurry?" Nana asked. "No time for seconds, eh?"

"I haven't fed Simon yet."

"You have plenty of time," Nana insisted. "Eat."

Tata, who was pouring coffee, twitched his bushy eyebrows up and down. "Hey, Kiko. Since when you so eager to go to school? She must be cute."

I caught myself from saying, *She is*, thinking about Daphne. Instead I wiped a smile off my face.

Tata pulled Nana's coarse shoulder-length hair aside and kissed the back of her neck. "Smells good."

Nana poked his big belly with her elbow. "Not in front of Kiko," she whispered and giggled.

Tata scooped up a rice and egg tortilla. He settled on a kitchen chair and tipped the chrome legs backward. "What about Tatan?"

Nana pulled black knobs off the stove. "I'll work harder at making the house safe. You put locks on the sheds, no? And those nice navy men said, 'No more land mines,' eh? What else can he get into? We'll just make it safe so Tatan will be all right until Kiko gets home."

She handed me a block of knives from the counter and a handful of steak knives from the drawer. "Please lock these in the shed. Anyt'ing else?"

I sighed and took the knives. "How about we hire a nurse?"

"We sunk everyt'ing we had into the shop," Tata said.

Nana twisted her ring. "That and buying this house two years ago."

If I didn't get out of there, Nana would have me rearranging the whole kitchen. "I got to slop Simon or I'll be late for school." I pulled from the fridge a can of leftovers—mostly corn and other vegetables—Nana had set aside for Simon. I darted for the door. "'Bye Nana. 'Bye Tata." I scooted through the screen door. Bobo jumped up and scratched my bare legs, 'cause I wear shorts to school.

"Kiko!" Nana hollered, then lowered her voice, probably so as not to wake Tatan. She followed me out the door. "Come home right away. No dawdling, you hear me?" She dumped a scoop of dog food into Bobo's dish outside. "And stay out of the boonies. Your Tihu Gabe found strange-looking shrimp traps in the river. Not like anyone around here would make. That's too close to where you play baseball as far as I'm concerned." The water from the spigot drowned out the rest of what she was saying. She turned it off after filling Bobo's water bowl.

I guess I could watch Tatan. Not like I'd be doing anything else after school. After locking up the knives in the shed with Tatan's machete, I waved at Nana. Bobo followed me down the dirt lane but stopped at the end where I turned out of sight toward the bus stop.

When Tomas and I arrived at school, the whole place was buzzing about more than what everybody got for Christmas.

"Did you hear about Kiko Chargalauf?" the students said in the halls. "Heard he was arrested! . . . No, it was his tata, Ferdinand . . .

Well, I heard they both got arrested, and thrown in jail, after they lobbed a live grenade at some tourists. . . . "

"Forget them." Tomas placed his hand on my shoulder.

I might have taken Tomas's advice, but my eyes were glued on Daphne chattering away by her locker with a bunch of girls from our sophomore class. Great. Just what I needed. Her telling everyone she saw my crazy tatan naked at *Las Posadas*. Just my luck, Tatan would have to run naked in front of Mary the Mother of God. I'd threatened the boy who played Joseph I'd beat him up if he told. But Daphne? Would she tell? I was too embarrassed to ask. Still, I had a right to know.

I walked over to Daphne, Tomas keeping pace with me, and asked, "Can I talk to you?" I looked at the other twittering girls who had hushed, and added, "Privately."

The giggling started up again but the girls moved on down the hall and left Daphne and me alone, except for Tomas.

I studied her brown eyes. She didn't shy away for once and held my gaze steady. I realized I was holding my breath. I let it out. "Have you told anyone about my tatan?"

At first she looked puzzled. When I said, "At *Las Posadas*, when you came to our house as Mary," a flicker of recognition lit in her eyes.

"You didn't tell, did you? About Tatan." The bell rang. The halls were emptying.

Daphne scowled. "You'd think that of me? Then you don't know me at all!"

Hurt, anger—it all crossed her face. Then the worst of it, tears welled up in Daphne's eyes. The bell rang again. The halls were empty except for us. Tomas was at my elbow saying, "Let it go, man. We got to get to class." He left.

Daphne wiped her eyes and ran off to class. I stood there so long I had to go to the office and get a tardy slip.

I had trouble concentrating in class. Between trying to figure out how I could talk to Daphne again and straighten things out, and wondering what Tatan was up to, I kept staring at the clock. By lunchtime I was torn about whether to go to the cafeteria and find Daphne, or go to the office and ask to call home. I went to the office first. Tatan didn't answer the phone.

I rushed to the cafeteria, but Daphne was already gone. Tomas wasn't at our regular table either. I couldn't find my lunch money, then realized I forgot to get it from Tata that morning. So I left the lunchroom without eating.

Later in history class, the guy in front of me kept nodding off, his head bobbing up and down like a fishing cork. I was so tired from going to bed late, then not sleeping good, that I could have slept too. I wish they gave us *siestas* like in the old days. The open jalousie windows didn't do any good this time of year. Guam was the same temperature year 'round—82 degrees. But at this time of the year it rained a lot. Since it wasn't raining today, just threatening to, it was so muggy I could have sliced the air with a knife, like slicing sea cucumbers for sushi.

I rubbed my eyes and rifled through my Guam history book. I needed to do something to stay awake while our teacher droned on, sounding like the bomber Sammy navigated. I flipped to a chapter we hadn't gotten to yet: "THE JAPANESE OCCUPATION, December 10, 1941, to July 21, 1944."

. . . *Concentration camps, forced labor, Merizo massacre, beheadings, rapes . . .*

I put my finger under the word *rapes*.

There were war stories in the newspaper every July during Liberation Day, but I never read about any rapes before.

I read over the section a second time to see if any names were mentioned, like there would be if it were a newspaper article about a crime committed nowadays. The only names I could find were of martyrs and heroes.

The *manamkos*, when they told stories of long ago, they were good things, happy things, funny things that happened. If they talked of war, it was bragging rights about who was a hero, and who hid

George Tweed, that American G.I. radioman, the longest, and who sneaked out in his hidden canoe and warned the Americans first of key Japanese positions.

When the reporters wrote of war, it was those happy-ending stories that named people's names in them. The kind of stories kids clipped and took to school for show-and-tell when they were little because they were proud their tatan and nana bihus were heroes.

But not bad stuff. Not stories about murders, and people getting their heads chopped off, and people with body parts blown up by grenades the Japanese threw at unarmed Chamorros in Merizo caves. Those people were all dead. No one reported their names. Not the textbooks, not the newspapers. Not unless they came out alive or a hero.

Bad stories didn't list names. Not stories about . . . about rape. No one came out a hero in those stories. No one. And who wanted to read that they were a *mestizo*, mixed-blood, because some man raped their nana? Who wanted his nana's name in the history book under a bold subtitle:

WOMEN RAPED

Tragedies happened to No Names. Not to people you knew. Not to your family. Especially not to your nana—

"Kiko!" my *haole* history teacher called.

I swear my body jumped a foot off the chair. I checked the rest of the class and realized I was practically the only one awake. "What?"

"Name the four colonial powers that have ruled Guam since Ferdinand Magellan discovered the Mariana Islands in 1521."

I sighed, then rattled off on auto-pilot what every Guamanian knows, "Spain, United States, Germany, and Japan." I looked out the jalousies and thought how never again would the words in my history book be just dry, lifeless facts, but rather real things that happened to real people. People I knew.

*

I checked the mailbox when I got home from school. Bills and ads, that's all there was. No letter from Sammy. How hard could it be to scribble on a postcard and pop it into a mailbox? Sammy wasn't good about writing home when he was away at engineering school or air force training either. Why would he worry Nana like this? Didn't Sammy know he's her favorite son? If Nana had her way, Sammy would never have left Guam. Now I got to be the one to see the disappointment on her face when she comes home to no letter from Sammy.

I went in the house, dropped the mail on the kitchen counter, and found Tatan sacked out on the couch with the TV still on. I turned off *M*A*S*H* and he woke up, which wasn't what I had intended.

Tatan stood up and seemed to have trouble walking across the living room. He complained his muscles were sore, and didn't know why. I knew it must be from digging all those holes, but wasn't about to remind him.

He followed me into the kitchen and practically fell into the kitchen chair, he had such trouble bending. I opened the fridge to get a snack. I found some chicken legs left over from the potluck. I slapped a cold chicken leg and cole slaw on a plate for Tatan, too, and put it on the table in front of him. He made a face and griped about not being able to use the stove. "It no work."

I didn't want to get into that again. And there was no way I'd fire up the outside grill just for an after-school snack. Nana should be home in a couple of hours and she would heat up a warm dinner.

Tatan picked at his chicken, not really eating any of it. I finished two chicken legs and was polishing off a heap of slaw when Tatan put his plate in the sink and looked out the window. "Who in blazes dug those holes in our yard? Want we should fall in and break our necks like chickens for dinner?"

How could he honestly not remember? It was only two nights ago! I stood there with my teeth in my mouth, as my nana bihu used to say, and shook my head.

Tatan turned and roared, "Kiko! Fill in those holes!" I didn't move. "Now, I say!"

*

It was the second week of January, on a Thursday to be exact, when I knew I couldn't stall any longer; I had to fill the holes. Nana asked two things every day first thing when she got home from work: "Any mail from Sammy?" and "Did you fill in those holes yet?"

When I pleaded I was too busy to shovel dirt, she'd say, "I don't see you studying your Catechism."

Tata said, "Your arm's not broke," when I whined I didn't want to. Finally, Tata threatened, "You're grounded until you do it!"

I knew once Tata got that tone of voice I'd better do whatever it was I was told or I would be grounded for real. "No ifs, ands, or buts about it," as Nana would say.

So, since I intended to play baseball with Tomas that weekend, I knew by Thursday I'd better start packing those holes with dirt. And maybe, just maybe, I could get Tatan to help me. Provided Bobo didn't dig the dirt out faster than we filled it back in.

Bobo wasn't waiting for me when I got home Thursday. That was odd. Oh well, Bobo was getting old. Maybe he didn't hear me coming.

"Tatan." I shuffled my zoris off inside the door.

"Tatan." I dropped my notebook onto the kitchen table.

"Tatan," I called louder. Still no answer.

I opened the refrigerator. I didn't find anything to eat so I opened a can of Spam, sliced it, and put it between white bread spread with mayonnaise. Nana wasn't home so I glugged milk straight from the carton.

"Tatan!" I called as I searched throughout the house. He wasn't sleeping on the couch or his bed. He wasn't watching TV or listening to the radio. He wasn't in the bathroom. Maybe he was out back with Bobo.

I slipped my zoris on, went outside, and ran around the house, looking as far as I could in every direction.

No Bobo. No Tatan. Maybe he went to a neighbor's.

I decided to get the shovels out of the shed since I was already outside, then go back in the house and call some neighbors. I headed for the tool shed to fetch the key Tata had hidden, taped above the door ledge. No need for a key. Someone had busted the lock open. There was a good-sized rock with fresh chip marks lying on the ground. I opened the shed.

What was missing? I searched the shadows. What?

Tatan's machete!

I ran out of the shed and around the yard in a frenzy, whistling and calling, "Tatan! Tatan! Bobo! Here, boy, come!" My pig squealed and butted against his pen. I stuck two fingers in my mouth and let a high-pitched whistle rip, hoping Bobo would hear it and come running home, bringing Tatan with him.

No Bobo. No Tatan.

I thought about calling my parents, but decided, not yet. It'd take them so long to get to Talofofo from Tumon at thirty-five miles an hour that Tatan might be home by then. I'd have worried them for nothing.

Should I call neighbors?

After just having had all the neighbors over because of the bomb scare, I didn't want to be like the boy who cried wolf every time my tatan turned up missing. Besides, it was still daylight. There were a few hours left to look for Tatan and Bobo before dark. I'd look for Tatan myself first.

I tried hard to think of where they could be. Tatan didn't have a car anymore. We lived too far to walk to a store. To the west of us were boonies and the river leading to Talofofo falls and mountains. To the east were cliffs descending to the beach at Talofofo Bay. Our neighbors lived north. And the road led south. Where would Tatan have gone?

I guessed it depended on whether Tatan's mind was in the present or the past when he left. If Tatan and Bobo followed the road then I would have seen them from the bus window. If Tatan went toward the Pacific Ocean, he couldn't get into too much trouble that way. Besides, it was quite a hike down to the bay. If Tatan took his machete, and if he was in his right mind, chances are he'd take it to whack through boonies. I decided to search through the boonies first.

While it was still daylight . . .

I took a sickle from the shed to slice through the underbrush. I ran to the river opening past where Tomas and I play ball.

I followed the river.

"Tatan!" I stopped and whistled again. "Bobo. Here boy. Come!"

Frogs croaked, trees creaked, lizards chirped, and water gurgled downstream. But no sound of Tatan or Bobo. Where were they? I whacked at the weeds and smacked swarms of mosquitoes that felt as if they were eating me alive.

Twigs and bramble thorns poked and tore at my feet and ankles. When I walked by the marshy bank, red mud oozed around my zoris and rocks jabbed through to the soles of my feet. Should I go back to the house and put on jeans and gym shoes?

Fading sunrays sunk behind the trees. "No time." I pressed on, calling Tatan and Bobo's names until my throat grew sore.

I had to try a new tactic. I sickled through the underbrush toward a banyan tree. I finally reached the vine-like roots growing above ground around its mother tree. I gingerly latched onto roots, not wanting to disturb spirits that haunted the banyan. "Steady now, I just want to climb you. I promise not to break one branch."

I climbed the giant to peer out from beneath its leafy head. When I was fairly high up I cupped my hands around my mouth like a megaphone and hollered, "Tatan! Bobo! Tatan!"

I listened. No voice nor bark.

I shifted my body and climbed around the tree, spiraling downward, pausing every few steps to stop, search, and call again, "Tatan! Bobo! It's me, Kiko! Where are you?"

"What's the use? I'm going hoarse." I climbed down and dropped to the ground. Still no answer echoed back.

I pressed on toward the falls. I kept trying to push horrible thoughts out of my head. *Is Tatan so far gone he'd stumble over the falls? What if he went toward the ocean instead and plunged down the cliff? Nana will die if anything happens to Tatan! It will drive her over the edge with Sammy gone, too.*

Sunlight slanted lower, and dimmer. I stepped in deer droppings and pig manure. Any other day I would have stopped and scrapped the crap off my zoris. "No time." I whacked the daylights out of the weeds, not caring that a thorn vine snapped back and ripped my leg. "That's the penance I pay for not taking seriously Tatan's dementia." Lizards scurried past my feet. Coconut crabs shuffled through leaves on the jungle floor. Roaches and beetles dove under rocks. "That's it. Get out of my way you! Get out of my way!" I screamed. "Where *are* they?" Now I was the one crazy out of my mind.

No sign of human life . . . until I reached a bamboo thicket. The forest floor seemed mashed down. I don't know why, but I looked to see if the whacked-up snake was still there. *Nada.*

I raised my sickle and swung it down and back up, making half-moon slices. I tromped through the underbrush to move back toward the river. One cut close to the ground hacked up a chunk of coconut fibers woven like a monstrous spider web. I jumped back and fell on my butt. "Whoa! I could've been strung up like a boonie deer." I marveled at the trap. "Who put that there?"

Chicken skin raised on my arms. An eerie feeling settled over me like mist in the morning. I felt clammy and . . . watched.

Those were no *taotaomona* spirits. Someone had been there. I felt it in my gut.

I didn't wait to find out who it was. I dashed into the boonies, not slowing to sickle the brush, sword grass cutting my legs. I ran so fast mosquitoes couldn't land on me.

In the distance, I heard water rushing over a cliff.

I raced until my side cramped and I doubled over, gasping for breath.

Ha, ha, ha, ha, something panted beside me.

I jumped so hard I felt akin to a molting snake shedding its skin.

"Bobo! Don't scare me like that!" I bent to hug my dog's neck. Bobo, slobbering, licked sweat off my face.

"Where's Tatan, boy? Where's Tatan? Go get him, boy!" My throat scratched just saying it.

Bobo loped through the brush. When Bobo barked I followed him, all the while calling, "Tatan! Tatan!" Finally I spotted Tatan, dressed in khakis, barely visible in the haze of dying daylight.

"Antonio?" Tatan peered at me from under his hand hooding his eyes.

Tihu Tony? Nana'd told me that I looked like her brother in California. *Does he t'ink I'm Tihu Tony?* "It's me, Kiko."

"Of course. What do you t'ink I am? Stupid, eh?" Tatan dropped his hand from over his brow and straightened his spine. "What's the fuss?"

"I couldn't find you, Tatan. You or Bobo. I was worried somet'ing happened to you."

"What makes you t'ink I'm not okay? I been looking for boonie peppers, Bobo and me." Tatan patted bulging pockets. "And look!" Tatan held up three fruit bats. "Good eating tonight, eh?"

"Tatan! Have you been in the caves? The ones with the ancient Chamorro drawings? Is that why I couldn't find you? How could you do this to me? Scare me half to death?" It didn't matter that fruit bats boiled in milk are a delicacy, I felt like pounding something. Tatan couldn't go off like that on his own anymore. "Come on, let's go home. Now." I sliced the sickle through underbrush.

Tatan carried his fruit bats and stomped on ahead of me, mumbling, "Who do you think you are? Disrespecting *manamko*. I should check in with you where I go, eh? And smart-mouthing me like that. Young 'uns got no respect for elders these days."

I did a lot of mumbling, too, but not loud enough for Tatan to hear. My nana would have washed my mouth out with soap if she heard what I said. But I was mad, really mad. He scared me more than I'd ever been scared before.

CHAPTER 10

HUNGER

JANUARY 13, 1972

Still as a Buddha statue, Seto crouched in reeds by the river. Waiting . . . watching . . . knife poised. His heart raced like that of a hunted deer.

Aiee, close. Too close. Seto clasped his hand over his chest. *I must be careless in old age. I should have waited until nightfall. They could have seen me.* His father's voice repeated in his head, *Stupid. Careless.*

He parted reeds and peered out. *No one.* He looked again.

If I was not so hungry, I would go below.

Seto pulled a trap up, careful not to splash the water.

He planned to take a bath, but decided against it since men were trampling near his hiding place. He was missing traps. His net destroyed.

No shrimp, no fish, no eel. Not even a bit of algae floated into the few traps left.

Oh, to be free to go to the ocean. I long for salt, and kelp, and Ono— fish—and eel. Instead I am prisoner here. Afraid of beasts on two feet. Scared of my shadow that it might give me away. Frightened of spirits who visit by night. I hide underground by day like a rat. And scurry at twilight scrounging for food. My life has rotted here. What waste.

Seto lifted his other trap from the river.

Nothing.

His knife scraped white coconut meat into traps for bait.

To think I almost used this knife on that boy.

He lowered one trap back into water.

Would I break my vow to native ghosts not to murder again?

He put the second trap into water, then duck-walked through reeds, afraid to stand up after so close an encounter.

Would I have killed him like we did those other two unsuspecting natives who came upon our secret lair? The one I shot in haste, and my comrades carved with their knives?

Would I? Seto looked at his knife, his hands. He had hidden entangled in the roots of the spirit tree. He thought the boy saw him at first. As the boy climbed the tree Seto was tempted to reach his hand up and grab the boy by the ankle and rip him to the ground. Instead, he stood rooted, as if one with the tree. Listening to his calls like wind through the jungle. When the boy came down the tree, Seto stalked him.

Had not the old man come along with his dog, and bats, and pockets bulging with peppers?

Surely I could not have killed them both. My gun corroded. One of me. Two of them. And a dog.

His insides gnawed together, stomach rumbling like storm cloud warnings.

He passed up toadstools, for not being reared a country boy he knew not which mushrooms were edible and which poisonous.

There is a reason I have survived these twenty-eight years, fifteen underground.

He plucked a snail, then two, and three off a tree trunk. They clung to the bark, leaving iridescent slime trails where they resisted being pulled from safety. But once the stranger's hand held them air bound, each slug retreated into its shell and sealed its hatch.

He cupped his hand around a tan tree frog, being careful not to squash it.

Is this all? All I catch tonight? It is barely enough to stop nip, nip, nipping of sharks' teeth at my stomach walls. It is barely enough to fuel my body. No wonder my flesh has shrunken and I look like a walking skeleton.

Still . . . Seto squatted and spied beyond the bamboo shoots. *Dare I chance venturing to breadfruit trees? Aiee . . . Boy too close.*

His stomach grumbled.

His heart thumped, thu-thumped, thumped.

He opened the bamboo trap door. And lowered himself, with his meager three snails and one tiny tree frog, into his hovel to dine.

Aiee. What I wouldn't give to have caught dog alone. For dog, I made no vow.

CHAPTER 11

SLAUGHTER

JANUARY 13–14, 1972

"Don't slop your hog today," Tatan ordered the second I stepped foot in the door after school. "Just give him plenty water."

"What? You not going to slaughter Simon tomorrow. You can't!" My parents had warned me not to name the pig. But how could I not? Simon had been the runt of the litter. I thought of him as my pet.

"Can and will." Tatan waved his hand as if saying, *End of argument.* He got up and left the kitchen. His bedroom door slammed shut. End of argument.

When it came to slaughtering livestock, such as chickens, pigs, and cows, I found a way to make myself scarce. Before Tata started Sammy's Quonset Hut, our family farmed. Sammy wasn't much of the farming type, but he helped out better than me. When it came to killing a chicken even, I hid until the poor thing was cooked and on the dinner table. Usually Tatan or Tata killed the chicken. But for as long as I remember, which wasn't all that long since Sammy's thirteen years older than me, my brother helped with the big jobs, like once a year when our tata butchered a cow in the late fall.

Last year, when Sammy was stationed on Guam, he slaughtered a pig with Tatan and Tata. I stayed at Tomas's house for two days. We camped out in his backyard. I was afraid I'd come home and find Simon gone. Boy was I relieved to find out that Sammy's pig, Chester, was slaughtered instead. (Although, I'm the only one who named the animals.) Chester had been a mean hog that charged me when I slopped the pigs. But now, with Tata working in Tumon and

Sammy off to war, evidently Tatan had made his mind up I would learn something about butchering.

I sat on the front steps with Bobo, waiting for my parents to come home. Before Nana could ask if any mail from Sammy had arrived, I jumped up and pleaded with her, "Tatan's going to murder Simon tomorrow! Tell him 'Don't do it!'"

"Oh, don't be melodramatic." Nana petted Bobo's head. "I told you not to get attached. Tatan's butchering the pig for the fiesta in Tumon. We offered. Now, excuse me, Tatan called and said somet'ing about needing me to cook some bats?"

"But what about school?" I called after her.

"Missing one day won't hurt," Nana's muffled voice called back. I glanced through the screen and could see her shuffling through the mail, hoping for a letter from Sammy.

I scooted up to the stoop and leaned my back against the house to wait for Tata to finish whatever he was doing in the shed. Finally Tata walked up the two steps and opened the screen door. I sprung up between Tata and the door, and gripped his arm. "Do you really trust Tatan with knives? You know how he's been lately."

Tata glared at me. "I t'ink it's you who don't want to touch the knives, eh, Son? I'm not worried. Look around you." Tata spread his other hand toward the land, as if he were a priest blessing it. "Used to all be farmland. Your ancestors were farmers. Remember before we bought the shop, eh? We raised cows, hogs, and chickens. Tatan's been butchering since he was half your age. That's a long time ago. I'm not worried. He could slaughter in his sleep."

Bobo edged between my legs and tried to wiggle his way through the door. I let go of my tata's arm, bent down and wrapped my arms around Bobo's neck. Fine, if they wanted to be that way about it, I'd go out to the pig pen and not eat dinner either.

That night I lay in bed listening to rain falling on our tin roof. First, in tinkles. Then, like rocks pelting a window pane. I worried about where Bobo slept since he couldn't curl up under the porch like at our old house. I should've left the shed door open like I did before Tatan went crazy in the head.

Thunder rolled. Lightning cracked. I sat up, and looked out the window at a lightning bolt creasing the sky like a blue-white scar. I hated to admit it, but on nights like that I missed being a little boy again who curled up next to Sammy in bed. I slept with my big brother from the time I outgrew my crib until I was five. When Sammy graduated from high school our parents bought us two single beds. He wouldn't let me sleep with him anymore. He said we both needed to grow up since I was going to school and him to college. I started wetting the bed. I never told my parents it was because I missed sleeping beside Sammy. It was as if my security blanket had been ripped away from me.

In a fit of sleep, I finally dozed off.

Tatan woke me early. Tata and Nana had already left for work. Nana left refried rice with Spam in the refrigerator for breakfast.

"No stalling," Tatan said.

I didn't feel like rifling through the drawer for stove knobs so I ate congealed Spam and cold rice.

"Tatan, I'm not sure this is a good idea. I never helped slaughter before."

"Help? Help! Why, you won't be helping me slaughter."

"I won't?"

"Nada, not one bit."

"Really?"

"Really. I gonna teach you to do the whole t'ing yourself. Except where I got to help string him up," Tatan said. "Now, get going, boy. Time's a-wasting."

I pitched the rest of my breakfast in the trashcan. I put on gym shoes and dragged my feet out the door, letting it slam.

A wet and muddy Bobo scratched my legs.

It had rained so much all the holes brimmed with water. The sun blazed a yellow halo over blue skies.

"Yep, a good day for slaughtering." Tatan took a deep breath, then ambled on over to the tool shed as if he was out for a Sunday stroll after Mass. He stopped and raised his eyebrows as if to say, *You coming?*

For once, I wished I was at school instead. I slumped my shoulders, kicked the ground, and shuffled to the tool shed. Bobo drooped his tail between his legs. Tata not only hadn't replaced the broken lock, he had removed the lock on the curing shed as if giving his blessing to sacrifice Simon.

In the tool shed, Tatan waited with his arms folded across his belly as big as a watermelon. He had stripped his outer shirt down to his muscle-man T-shirt. Only his muscles had gotten flabby. I dug my hands into the pockets of my jean shorts.

We glared at each other. Neither of us budged. Bobo curled up on the dirt floor.

"Haven't got all day, boy. Get the tools."

I balled my fists and sunk them deeper into my pockets.

"Fetch the knife, stone, ropes, matches, propane torch . . . " Tatan named a list of tools as if he were dictating a grocery list.

I didn't know which knife Tatan meant so I picked up several, along with the whetstone and buckets.

Tatan reached to a top shelf high above his head. Hidden behind an oil can and a rusty bait bucket, he pulled out a gun. "You want to shoot or slit?"

I gave him the *atan baba*, evil eye.

"Fine," Tatan said. "I shoot. You slit. Next time we swap."

"Next time! Man, I can't wait 'til Sammy comes home."

"How you know next time won't be you and Sammy doing this together like two men?"

Men. Did I hear Tatan right? I didn't say nothing. Instead I dumped the supplies in buckets and carried them to the yard.

Tatan shut Bobo in the tool shed. "For his own good." Bobo scratched at the door.

Tatan threw dry sticks and charcoal under a huge black cast-iron cauldron propped above the fire pit. I lit the match and fire shot up under the vat filled with rainwater. When blue flames licked the cauldron, we walked over to Simon's pen.

I sat on the wooden fence and listened to Tatan as he explained how I should sidle up on Simon's back, real friendly like. "Don't spook him." Then, holding the knife in my stronger hand, slip my arm around his neck and bear my weight down as if I'm practically riding him bareback. "Keep your arm slung low and your head high, 'cause I aim to shoot him through the head, ear to eye. You got that?"

I couldn't believe this was happening. "What if you miss and shoot me instead?"

Tatan jabbed a knife in the air. "Trust me." He made a slicing motion to make his point.

I studied the ground as if looking for answers. Crap. Tata's at work. Sammy's flying over some Vietnamese jungle. Did I have a choice but to help? No. I'd have to trust him. Tatan's *manamko*. I'd have to be a man, like Sammy told me to be, no matter how I felt about Simon. There was no more hiding like a little boy.

"Ready?"

No way would I ever be ready, not for this.

"Do it."

I slid down off the fence and into the pen. I clutched a sharp long knife in my hand so tight it shook.

"Call him," Tatan whispered.

"Here piggy, piggy, piggy. Here piggy," I called hesitantly.

Simon grunted in the dirt, routing for buried morsels of food.

"Here piggy, piggy . . . "

"Boy. You can do better than that," Tatan growled. "Time to kill the beast."

I wished he'd quit calling me boy. Did Tatan think I was Sammy or Tony? I cleared my throat, spit on the ground. "My name's Kiko."

"Kill the beast," Tatan growled again, like he was totally focused on the pig, and the pig alone.

I charged after Simon and sang out, "Sou-EE. Sou-EE."

Startled, my pig broke through a downed fence slat I had put off repairing. I chased him into the yard, calling, "Sou-EE. Sou-EE."

I got close enough and grabbed his tail. He squealed and twisted in a circle. I leaped at Simon and belly-flopped into one of Tatan's foxholes.

Tatan roared with laughter. "You muddier than the hog ever was."

"Very funny. Ha. Ha." I climbed out of the hole, sopping wet. "I could've hurt myself, 'specially holding this knife." I checked myself out to make sure I wasn't bleeding anywhere. "Look, I ruined my only gym shoes."

"They wash." Tatan's chest heaved up and down again from chuckling.

Bobo barked from inside the shed.

"This is all a big joke to you, isn't it?" I'd show Tatan not to laugh at me. I planted both feet firmly on the ground. I placed my hands—one holding the knife blade down—on bent knees.

"Here piggy, piggy, piggy," I called softly. I chanted louder, "Sou-EE. Sou-EE."

My pig wandered over to the side of the shed and snorted. Bobo yapped non-stop. Yellow-tipped paws peeked out from underneath as he tried to dig his way out.

I bolted up and hollered, disgusted. "For the love of Pete . . . Simon!"

When I called his name he trotted over to me, expecting to be fed. I stroked Simon's back. He nuzzled my hand, smelling for corn or an apple core. I massaged behind Simon's ears. I slipped up behind my pig, melded my body on top, and embraced his neck. He smelled earthy, of mud and mildew and potato peels.

Tatan grabbed my hair and yanked my head back. *Bang!*

Judas! For a split second I thought he'd shot me. But I must still be alive, my heart was drumming on my chest. Instead the bullet had entered behind Simon's left ear and exited through his right eye.

Simon dropped to the ground. His body writhed in spasms. Tatan straddled the pig and grabbed his front feet to keep them from kicking me.

I could tell from Tatan's red face he was yelling, but his voice sounded dull and muffled because the gunshot had deafened my hearing.

Watching Simon convulsing, I just wanted to put him out of his misery. I felt for the tip of the breastbone like Tatan had told me to do. I couldn't watch. I closed my eyes and stabbed the blade below Simon's jaw. I opened my eyes and watched myself thrust the knife upward as if someone else were killing my pig, not me.

"Spill his blood!" Tatan ordered.

No blood. Not deep enough.

I plunged the blade in until the handle sunk in Simon's fatted chest. I ripped the knife upward. Warm, maroon blood gushed once I severed the main artery. I looked down at my own blood-drenched body and vomited.

"Wash off later," Tatan said. "Get the cart."

I wanted to be done with it. Maybe go wash in the river deep in the boonies. Get away from there. I wheeled a wooden pull-cart from behind the house. Back when our family farmed the land, a carabao—water buffalo—pulled the cart.

Tatan was right, no way he could lift this two hundred-pound pig onto the cart. It did take two men. After Tatan and I grunted and pulled and lifted the pig into the cart, I picked up the handle and hoisted the wooden beams across my shoulders. As if I were a beast of burden, I hauled dead Simon over to a tree.

In the Ifil tree near the boonies hung a block and tackle dangling from a sturdy branch. Tatan tossed me a thick rope. "String him up."

I threaded the rope through the come-along. I tied one end of the rope around Simon's back legs. I jumped, choked up on the other rope, lifted my knees waist-high, and swung my body down full force like a bell-ringer in a church tower.

I was too lightweight.

Tatan stretched up, clasped my hands in his, and together we yanked the rope down and pulled the pig up. I secured the rope around the trunk of the tree. Tatan doubled the knot.

Tatan set buckets underneath the pig. He pointed to its anus. "Cut here. Not too deep . . . Stinks."

Yeah, right, as if I could stink any worse than I already did with blood and vomit on me.

I stabbed the knife point in little up-and-down incisions around the butt hole. When I freed the rectal canal Tatan reached in and worked feces back toward the intestine with his hands. He was explaining the whole time what he was doing. "Here, tie this off," he said when he finished.

"What with?" I asked.

"String."

"I didn't get any. It wasn't on your list."

"Have you no sense? Get somet'ing to tie it off. Be quick about it!"

I hated when he talked to me like a stupid little boy. I searched in the cart, on the ground, and around the tree. No string.

Flies buzzed Tatan's hands as he held the smelly mess. "Hurry up!"

I looked at the underbrush at the jungle's edge. My thoughts drifted as I spied plumeria and hibiscus. Oh, to have my nose buried in those flowers. I took off toward the hibiscus shrub.

"Where's your head, boy!" Tatan shouted. "Don't leave me stranded."

I brought back bark from the hibiscus that I'd shredded into jute-like string. "Look, Tatan, pago thread."

I wasn't for sure, but I thought Tatan muttered, "Good t'inking," which would've been high praise from him. I tied the butt hole with the string I'd made, careful not to get any stink on me.

"What next?"

"That." Tatan pointed to the pig's penis.

Ouch. Poor Simon.

"Good t'ing he's dead, eh?" Tatan tried to chuckle, but it came out more as one low grunt.

"Yeah, heh, good t'ing."

Tatan pointed to where I needed to insert the blade. First I cut through the skin and fatty tissue on each side of the penis, then underneath the penis along the middle of the pig's belly.

"Now pull his, you know, ding dong, and that other flap of skin up between his legs and *schliitt*." Tatan made a slicing motion with his finger.

I winced, then cut off Simon's penis.

"Okay. You done good. Now, get the bigger butcher knife. You gonna crack the breast bone."

I couldn't believe I was really doing this. I fetched a butcher knife out of a bucket. I set my bloodied knife in the tree. I thrust the butcher knife in the neck opening where I had slit Simon's throat, and with hard upward thrusts I jerked the blade from neck to pelvis.

Tatan shoveled buckets under the pig as it spilled its guts.

"Not too deep," he warned, "or you burst the . . . " Tatan skipped back.

Oh no, I punctured the bladder! I jumped back. Crap. Too late. Urine sloshed out, the first cleansing fluid to wash away Simon's blood from my hands. "Grr-ross." I slung the pee from my hands, then wiped them on weeds. I gasped in short breaths through my mouth, trying not to smell myself.

"Ha. Ha . . . Ha. Ha," Tatan laughed. "Happened to me a lot when I first butchered."

It was pretty funny, thinking about Tatan as a young boy learning how to slaughter his first pig and being initiated with urine. So I found myself kind of snorting a laugh or two.

"How old were you?" I asked.

"What?"

"How old? When you killed your first pig?"

Tatan thought a moment. "Twelve. No, that Sammy. Maybe I six."

"Six!"

"Yeah, it was our turn for fiesta. My tata decided it was time I learned. 'Course I was too small for lifting. And he too embarrassed for me to touch the, you know . . . "

"Ding dong?"

Tatan's face turned as red as his bandana. "You talk too much. Besides, we stink plenty bad. Let's finish the beast."

I was glad he was having a good day, a clear day in his mind. Maybe he was getting better, eh? I'd be sure and tell Nana, give her hope. She needed something to cheer her up, always worrying about Tatan and Sammy.

Together, we finished gutting our pig. Tatan moved the buckets and I positioned the wagon under the pig. Tatan cut the rope. My knees buckled as I shouldered the pig alone until Tatan joined me in easing the pig down into the wagon.

I pulled the wagon in front, and Tatan pushed from behind. We eased the pig into the cauldron of scalding water. Tatan tossed limes in the water; I scattered ashes. Tatan showed me how to pull at the hair to test when it was ready for slipping. What a pain in the butt. I never knew pigs had so much hair. Once we stripped hair off the front legs, we pulled the pig out and immersed his rear end into the hot water.

We scraped that pig bald.

"There, ain't he a t'ing of beauty?" Tatan remarked after we strung up our pig in the curing shed.

"He sure is." And I meant it. I admired the clean carcass from his curly tail down to the tips of his cloven hoofs, swaying on a rope from the rafters. Hanging upside down, Simon's flesh stretched out, his underside almost looked polished with his ribs gleaming. His ears were intact, except for a small bullet hole behind one ear that was barely visible with the blood washed off. Simon's eyes . . . I shut his eyelids. Simon's round snout was undisturbed.

And his mouth, gaping, ready to place a Rome Beauty apple in when he would be served on the fiesta banquet table.

"He sure is a beaut." I swallowed to get past the lump in my own throat.

"How'd it feel to do a man's job?"

I picked up a rag and wiped blood off my arms and hands. Is this what separated men from boys? Slaughtering the sacrificial pig? Like some ancient tribal ritual? Slitting throats and spilling blood?

"Before fiesta," Tatan said, "we come back and scrape maggots off him."

I decided right then and there I would never name another animal.

CHAPTER 12

RITE OF PASSAGE

JANUARY 13–14, 1972

A monsoon raged above Seto's cave. Pain seared through the marrow of his bones. His swollen joints throbbed. His head ached. The dank earth smelled of mildew and smashed snails.

Water seeped through hatch and chimney. He worried the roof would collapse. Or would water fill up his cave and drown him?

Seto climbed out of his grave naked. Better to face driving rain than drown underground like a rat. Besides, this might be a good night for hunting. At very least no natives would be out in thunder and lightning.

Seto caught frogs—many frogs, big frogs. The frogs jumped and squeaked and fought to get out of his burlap bag. Seto knew that suffocating feeling of wanting to be free. But his hunger proved stronger than his pity for captive frogs.

He took refuge among spirit tree roots until rain lessened.

Once underground he could not get a fire going. His fire sticks were damp. *What a waste*, Seto thought. He had finally caught dinner but could not cook it. There were many things Seto would eat raw—fish, snails, even eels—but not frogs.

He lay down on a wet mat to the sound of thrashing, squeaking frogs. Seto laid his arm against his throbbing head, and waited until his sticks dried.

Time was indiscernible underground. But that night, each second listening to rain and frogs was agony. Rain sounded like bullets firing overhead. Frog squeals turned to soldiers screaming. Seto curled into a ball, covered his head and ears, and cowered in his foxhole.

He could stand it no longer. If he ate frogs, the screams would stop and his ghostly comrades would leave him alone. He got up and struck two rocks together. Again. Again. A spark flashed. Seto pushed the rocks closer to paper and oil and struck them together furiously until a flame ignited his stove. Smoke roared out and choked him. The fire died. There would be no frog dinner tonight.

Hungry, exhausted, Seto coughed in spasms until he could do nothing but lay helplessly on the ground. His cave sweltered like a sauna. He pulled over his body moist newspapers and the only blanket he owned—one drab scratchy army blanket he had retrieved from the *Amerikan* dump. It had been so long ago Seto could barely remember living in the open. There was a certain comfort at times being cocooned in a tunnel. This was not one those times. His blanket weighed heavy on his body. Everything felt clammy, and stunk of burnt coconut oil and urine and mold.

As he lay still with the itchy blanket over his head, Isamu Seto tried to transport his mind to a pleasant memory of a time of winter when he shivered so bad his teeth clattered and goose bumps rose on his flesh. Such coldness with its crisp dry air might be welcome compared to the steamy jungle.

There were many winter days to choose from, having grown up in Japan. There were fond memories of snowball fights with classmates on the long walk home from school, and ice fishing with his Uncle Kenta Seto who drank too much *sake*. He had loved his uncle, who could be funny when not fighting with Isamu's father. Finally, Father forbade Isamu to ever see his uncle again. He knew not why, only that his father said Kenta shamed their family name. His father's stony heart never forgave, nor did he speak to his brother again.

Other less fond memories crept in; memories when lakes froze and Isamu Seto went on ice runs one winter for his mother. That frigid winter of ice storms, it became Seto's responsibility to cut ice blocks from the lake and haul them out with tongs to a sled. He slung leather straps over his shoulders and pulled ice blocks to his home. Curled in his cave, Seto's shoulders ached and feet felt numb as he remembered that cold winter. Seto buried his head under the army blanket, then took deep practiced breaths—in, out, in, out—to feel moisture warm his nose and cheeks.

Surely there was a more pleasant memory of ice and snow and cold. One that would warm his heart and settle his soul in this frog-screaming, smoke-filled grave.

Ah, hai, Seto thought about the time the priest had gathered him and his classmates in an ancient purification ritual. It was January and Seto had turned twelve the summer before. He would be a man soon, but he needed to prove himself first.

Snow blanketed his village and wind howled against his door like an evil intruder. Still, Seto stripped down to his loincloth and ran outside to battle the elements. New-fallen snow and ice formed a crust that stung Seto's feet as he stomped to the shrine to join his classmates. When he arrived other boys were jumping around, trying to get warm.

(An image of leaping frogs threatened to pull him out of the shrine and into his cave again, but Seto frowned, burrowed deeper into his blanket, and imagined red columns on a shrine. It was not difficult to remember what the bitter cold felt like.)

He had been embarrassed, standing in his loincloth exposing his pale scrawny limbs. This had been the winter before he hauled ice. Instead he had spent hours after school helping his father. A tailor shop is not a place to build brawny muscles, not like the son of a farmer or logger or builder.

The priest called for the boys to gather around him. For Seto, it was as if his name was the only one being called. Yet he felt intimidated when the priest held a wooden icon aloft. *"Ichi, ni, san, shi . . ."* Seto could not really say whether or not the priest had said the numbers first as a prelude to tossing the statue. But as Seto lay on his *tatami* underground, it comforted him to hear a voice—any voice, even his own—call out the warning numbers to give him a chance to retrieve the statue.

Instead, Seto would always wonder, what if he had been swifter, pushed harder, actually grabbed the statue and held on for dear life? Would he have been strong enough to climb the rope with it and ring the bell? His father might have been proud of him. Yet Seto could not climb the rope on the school grounds. Everyone knew it. Even when his headmaster caned his legs, it did not make his arms strong enough to pull his own weight to the top of the rope that hung from a tree.

It was not that Seto did not try to retrieve the statue. He did. At least he thought he did. Boys jostled and shoved him. Frigid water doused him. None of it made him strive to overcome his timidity. And then there was the loincloth. He must not have tied it tight enough because without his trousers to keep it in place, the cloth felt as if it was slipping, slipping. Seto kept tugging up the white strip covering his emerging manhood.

In the end, Mori, the butcher's son, retrieved the icon, climbed the rope, and rang the bell at the top of the shrine. Afterward, Seto ran with all the boys down to the lake where they plunged through rippling caps and submerged beneath icy water.

Seto shook uncontrollably at the memory. When he had tried to emerge again, he came up underneath ice. He pressed his face against ice and gasped air from pockets. He swallowed water and his lungs burned as he kicked and swam for an opening. Finally he burst free, breeching the surface like a whale being hunted by whalers.

The rest of his classmates were already on shore, wrapped in white sheets like burial cloths and being blessed by priests. Seto was last to resurrect from a watery grave and come to shore. He almost missed the blessing.

"Domo . . . " he whispered as he did so many years before. Seto craved the blessing from the priest. For a boy needs to be tried, purified, and blessed to become a worthy man.

The memory was a sad but fulfilling one. Seto fell into a deep, deep sleep. Later, as he fought between sleep and wake, he heard muffled squeals. At first he thought it was frogs still struggling to be free. But this frightful squeal was faint, yet shrill.

Seto sat up and listened closely. His heart raced. Could it be he caught something in his snare?

Bang!

Seto clutched his chest at the sound of gunfire. No more squeals. Silence. The suspense of not knowing was killing him.

CHAPTER 13

FIESTA

JANUARY 15, 1972

Simon looked very handsome dressed for dinner. Our smoked pig lay on the banquet table between kelaguen shrimp and ginger chicken.

Tasted good, too. I snatched a piece of pork from near the ribs. I smeared the grease from my mouth on the back of my hand and wiped it on my black trousers before pinching a shrimp. Tatan swiped a taro tip from the table. He was still on a roll, having a good day. Maybe Nana had gotten it wrong about his *lytico-bodig* growing worse. Maybe like Tatan had it wrong about Nana being raped. I closed my eyes and shook my head, trying to get all this crazy thinking to go away. I couldn't deal with it. This was going to be a fun night. Fiesta. Why ruin it by thinking too much?

"Boys!" Nana hissed. I downed the shrimp and scooted out of Nana's reach before she playfully swatted my hand. Tata laughed.

I heard Daphne giggling with the women and girls dressed in long flowered Filipina dresses. I still had not had a chance to explain and clear things up. She'd been busy getting her project ready for the science fair. So that cut out lunch hours. Then I was stuck rushing home after school every day to check on Tatan. Maybe tonight we could talk. I bent forward enough to look down the table. Daphne was stirring ambrosia, the nectar of the gods. I raked my fingers through my hair. Daphne glanced sideways at me. Could she guess I had it bad for her? Just looking at her in that yellow dress gave me a rush.

I was getting ready to go talk to Daphne when Nana said, "Tata's waiting for you. Get down to the procession." I hesitated and sniffed the lemon Nana was squeezing over tuna. "I'll join you later," she said.

I looked at Daphne again. Was she smiling at me? I chucked my chin and took off for the procession.

Tatan, Tata, and I hitched a ride in the back of a pickup to the other end of the beach. We joined thousands of Catholics gathered to honor Diego Luis de San Vitores, a Spanish Jesuit missionary. A Chamorro chief ordered him beheaded four hundred years ago because the priest baptized the chief's baby daughter without his permission. I guess I could see both sides. Nobody should go against the chief, especially not concerning his own family. But the priest was probably worried about the baby's soul if she died. It'd be a hard call. But beheading? Whoa, that's some seriously deep doo-doo. I wouldn't want to mess with any of that chief's daughters.

The pickup parked beside nuns. I never got why people called them penguins. Not that I've ever seen a penguin. But the nuns looked like a pod of dolphins in their gray cloaks.

"Care if I find Tomas, eh?"

"Go ahead," Tata said. "We'll see you at Saint William's Chapel."

I squinted into the setting sun, looking for Tomas. Padre Flores led the faithful down Tumon beach, his large gold cross beating against his chest steady as a drumbeat. Behind him twelve robed altar boys cupped their hands around candles. I imagine in the olden days they would have been carrying tiki torches. The tallest boy hoisted high a teakwood cross perched on a staff.

Ah, there was Tomas, walking behind the monks in brown robes, crunching seaweed and crushed coral under their sandals. I ran to catch up to Tomas, and my thin black tie—more like a noose Nana made me wear—flapped over my shoulder.

"Hey, bro," Tomas said, "seen Daphne? She's looking mighty fine."

I flicked my eyebrows, then looked out over the ocean instead of at Tomas. I flushed hot every time I thought about Daphne possibly seeing Tatan naked. I had to quit thinking about it, especially during this holy procession. Communion fell before the fiesta feast, so I tried to put Daphne, looking fine, out of my mind. I didn't have time for confession tonight, and I didn't need to spend the night with a boner.

I craned my neck back to see Tata walking alongside Tatan.

"Who you looking for, eh?" Tomas said.

"Oh, Tatan."

"Don't worry none. He's probably back with the *manamkos* chewing the fat about old times and whose obit is in the paper." Tomas laughed.

"Yeah, you probably right. Tatan's kay-o. Besides, Tata's keeping an eye out for him."

Waves lapped the shore and amber streaked the sky. We marched onward like Christian soldiers to the grotto.

"Hail Mary, full of grace, the Lord is with thee," the priest chanted once we huddled at San Vitores's shrine.

I crossed myself. Tomas fingered the crucifix around his neck. We responded, "Holy Mary, Mother of God, pray for us sinners now and in the hour of our death. Amen."

Tomas's stomach rumbled. I started to laugh, but put my hand over my mouth.

Tomas tried to hold back snickering, too, but it snorted through his nose.

Daphne glanced over from across the aisle with her eyebrows knit together. I cupped a fist to my mouth like a conch shell. *Ga-humph,* escaped through my fist.

The priest droned on.

Daphne smiled shyly and Tomas nudged me with his elbow and smiled back at Daphne.

" . . . which gives food to the hungry," the priest recited.

I looked at Tomas, which set off his snickering again.

"The Lord sets prisoners free," we responded.

I flicked my eyebrows at Daphne.

She giggled into cupped hands, but I could see her eyes dancing. Man, she was beautiful. What I wouldn't give for one dance with her. Maybe I'd get lucky and work up the nerve to ask her. Then I could talk to her and set things right. I might even tell her I like her.

The priest said, "The Lord takes care of strangers."

I shifted my eyes and caught sight of Tata and Nana, responding, "The Lord comforts the fatherless and widows . . . "

"Praise ye the Lord," the congregation ended.

Finally, Communion. Then we could eat. Then the music and dance. Maybe then I could spend time with Daphne.

The Father placed on the altar one gold chalice and one thin wafer the size of a tortilla. Inside the chalice sloshed a liquid the color of Simon's blood.

Smoke billowed from an oil incense burner, anointing my hair and clothes and skin with scents of musk and sandalwood, like the musty smell after a rain.

Father blessed the Eucharist. He lofted the wafer high, " . . . with Christ's body . . . " He broke off a smidgen and ate. He raised the chalice and crossed himself. "With this blood . . . " and drank.

People filed forward two by two as ushers directed each from one pew, then the other.

I looked down at my feet and tried to think pious thoughts. I didn't notice until I reached the altar Daphne had fallen in step beside me.

She closed her eyes, crossed herself, opened her eyes and lifted her face toward the padre. He placed a tiny bit of wafer on her tongue. The priest broke off another piece for me. All I could think about was what a gecko-sized bite Daphne had nibbled from the host. The priest extended the wafer. I ate Christ's flesh.

I turned to watch Daphne's lips sip from the communal chalice.

The priest handed it to me. *Her mouth touched this.* I gulped.

"He who eats and drinks unworthily eats and drinks damnation unto himself."

Never before did Christ's body and blood stick in my throat. I wanted to spit out the wafer and wine. I felt dirty. What about Confirmation? What made me think I was good enough to be confirmed into the faith?

I walked down the aisle beside Daphne, close enough to whiff the plumeria blossom in her hair. I had to restrain myself from reaching over and holding her hand.

After Communion we were swept outside to fiesta under the canvas covering. No longer the solemn atmosphere of *novenas*—prayers for the dead—as noisy throngs of people crowded around tables overflowing with food.

I took a deep breath to smell the red rice stained with achiote seeds, finadene sauce, empanadas, lumpias, and Filipino noodles marinated in ginger, soy, and rice wine. My mouth watered at the sight of mangoes, papayas, guavas, breadfruit, coconuts, and tart little mountain apples that were pickled, baked, juiced, or offered whole and unspoiled.

But at the center of the fiesta, like a sacrifice on the altar, was smoked pig. My pig. Simon. I felt proud.

"Amen." Father finished the blessing prayer. "And dig in!"

The priest led the procession down the tables, pausing over each dish as if it were a rosary bead.

Daphne smiled at me and swayed her body to strains of ancient Chamorro music. *Butsu*—three-quarter waltzes—flowed sweetly from the mandolin, ukulele, guitar, accordion, and bass fiddle. I wondered if after we ate, would Daphne dance with me? If I worked up the courage to ask?

I twisted my neck around, looking for Tatan. I hadn't seen him at the shrine with my parents. He should've been there, sharing in eating pig with me. After all, we slaughtered him together, Tatan and me.

Tomas came up behind me and slapped between my shoulders. "What you standing here for, eh? Let's eat."

Tata was slicing Simon, and Nana cut up pies. I lightly backhanded Tomas in the stomach. "You go on, bro. Catch you later."

I searched the crowd for Tatan's pale blue *guayabera*—Filipino shirt. I passed tables where children pleaded for sweetbreads and cakes. I wanted him to be with me when we dished up our pig on our plates.

I pressed by politicians, though not without having to shake a number of hands and getting caught in a few arm-on-shoulder hugs. I nodded and bobbed my head past nuns. I slipped past my buddies checking out young Chamorritas, like how I checked out Daphne.

Finally, I thought I spotted Tatan wandering around a group of *maga'hagas*. The older matriarchs sat waiting for family to bring *manamkos* plates of food so they wouldn't be jostled in line.

"Tatan," I waved, motioning for him to join me. "Tatan San Nicolas!" I called again.

As I drew closer to where I thought Tatan was standing I heard one heavy-set *maga'haga* in an orange muumuu say, "Shame, eh? About Tatan San Nicolas."

Another *maga'haga* in a green dress printed with pineapples replied, "*Lytico-bodig*. Sad. Thought he might be husband material."

The orange muumuu *maga'haga* jiggled with laughter. Several women twittered.

Embarrassed, I tried to move past them and call for Tatan on the other side when Widow Muumuu said my nana's name.

"Poor Roselina, after all these years . . . people forgetting where Sammy came from . . . now Tatan dredging up how Rosie was . . . soiled by those nasty Japanese fellas."

"Do you know that for a fact?" said a *maga'haga* wearing a cowry shell lei.

"It's come out," Widow Muumuu assured the women. "Day he chased that Japanese man at the beach, I heard. Couldn't help but come out now that Tatan San Nicolas has *lytico-bodig*. A man can't hide anger forever."

"For sure," agreed Widow Pineapple. "A-ranting and a-raving about what happened to us all in World War II. Concentration camps, Merizo massacre, the . . . well, you know, like what happened to poor Roselina . . . of course, didn't happen to me . . . I hid mo'e better."

I moved closer. Widow Muumuu caught my eye and puckered her mouth into a sour lime shape. Her triple chin waddled. The other *maga'hagas* must have noticed me, too.

Widow Cowry Lei said, "Nice fiesta, eh? Lots of food."

I nodded, and stomped off. I wanted to shut them up. Shut them all up. I didn't care that they were *manamkos*. Old biddies. They had no business talking about my nana that way. Gossipy bunch of old *maga'hagas*. Didn't they have anything better to do? Did everybody know my nana was raped? What did they say about Sammy? I broke out in a sweat and it felt as if a tight band squeezed my forehead.

Out under the canopy of stars, lighted by moonbeams and paper Chinese lanterns, I breathed in burning citronella. My head spun along with people swaying and swirling to a kaleidoscope of music. I felt light-headed and about to pass out. I vaguely made out Tatan on the opposite side of the circle beside the ukulele player.

"The old ladies from days of old will eat betel nut," the musician called.

People responded, "They'll spit out the tobacco that stains their teeth . . . "

I inhaled until my chest swelled, then exhaled a deep sigh. I breathed deep again. I felt like I couldn't get enough air.

Tomas came and stood beside me, balancing a plate overflowing with food.

"Seconds?" I asked Tomas.

"Thirds." I dove my fingers into Tomas's plate. He pulled it away. "Haven't you eaten, bro?"

"No." The room spun around me.

Tomas gave me a puzzled look, then pushed his plate back toward me.

"Tell you what," Tomas said. "I'll give you this whole plate of food if you go ask Daphne to dance."

"What?" It was all I could do to keep standing.

"I saw you two eyeballing each other," Tomas said.

"We weren't eyeballing. You were snorting, and we couldn't stop laughing."

"Did not."

"Did so. You were snorting." I snorted warthog sounds through my nose. "Snorting like Simon before I slit his throat." I plucked a slice of pig off Tomas's plate and ate it.

Tomas glared at me. "I dare you dance with her."

I was too upset by what the *maga'hagas* said about Nana to dance with anyone. I wished Tomas would just leave me alone. I cackled like a madman. "Like a double-dog dare?"

Tomas shoved his plate at me. "If you won't, I will."

My insides churned. All night I had wanted to dance with Daphne. But not now. The timing had to be right. I couldn't dance with Nana on my mind. With what everyone said happened to her. *Soiled*, the *maga'hagas* had said. *Raped*, the history book had said. I shook my head, hard enough to rattle my brains. If I could have, I would have slapped the side of my head and knocked the bad thoughts out my ear.

But I didn't want any other guy dancing with Daphne. I'd ask her to dance when I was good and ready. I dropped his plate as my eyes followed Tomas across the dance area toward a group of giggling teenage Chamorritas. When Tomas asked her to dance, Daphne's eyelashes fluttered on her cheeks like moth wings. The other girls huddled and giggled, covering their pink-tinted lips. But all I could see was Daphne, with her full lips puckered like the underside of a shell, and her full hips swaying onto the dance floor.

Tomas and Daphne whirled frantically to the marimba-like music. No touching. Just a lot of twirling next to each other. Mid-stride, the band wound down and switched to a slow, soulful song about a Chamorrita who lost her love at war.

Surely Tomas would nod, say "t'anks," and head back to finish his plate off. He'd had his dance at my expense. He'd made his point. It was over. A bro would do this for his buddy.

When I raised my head to the dance floor again, there was my best friend with both arms around Daphne's delicate waist, and her hands resting on his broad shoulders.

The band tightened across my forehead. Sweat blinded my vision. All I saw was a slant-eyed Japanese man embracing a young Chamorrita.

I shut my eyes, pressed my warm hand against the lids, then looked again. The lovely Chamorrita's head rested lightly on the foreign shoulder. Were his lips brushing against her long black hair? Was he holding her too tight and she couldn't break free?

I squinted, thrust my neck forward, and saw that the Chamorrita's eyes were closed and a hint of smile played on the man's face as he held her close.

I lunged for him. "Get your filthy hands off her, you dirty Jap!"

He spun around and scowled at me. "What the . . . ?"

I grabbed him and raised my fist.

The rest was a blur. Daphne gasped and ran off the dance floor. I remember flailing my arms and cursing a blue streak until some men and my tata held me down.

"You're crazy, man! You've lost it!" Tomas shouted at me and stomped off.

"Kiko!" Tata yelled at me. "Stop it!" He slapped my face. Nana grabbed my arm. She was wailing and crying.

"Leave me alone." I shook them off and pulled away. My breathing was labored. I was suffocating.

Tatan showed up, looking like he was stoned. "Pilar? What's happened? Where's Rosie? Rosie all right? Who hurt Rosie? Why she crying?"

Nana put her hands on Tatan's face. "Shh, it's all right. Everyt'ing's going to be all right. We're going home now."

But it wasn't all right. It had never been all right. We'd only been kidding ourselves. I shook all over. Yeah, they gave me what I wanted. They all left me alone. Just stood and stared at me and left me shaking like some maniac who'd cracked. Now who's the crazy one?

I followed Nana, leading Tatan from the fiesta. She sat in the back of the Datsun while I climbed in front with Tata. I hugged the door and stared out the window into the night. Better to watch the waves, think about walking into the water until it was deep over my ears and I couldn't hear the band playing that frolicking song, or Daphne crying, or people gossiping. *Soiled. Raped.*

Tata started the engine, and ground the gears. He glared daggers at me. Why should I care? My heart had already been sliced with a machete. I just wanted to get the hell out of there.

When we got closer to home I stared into the boonies. Pretended I was wandering in the jungle until I got lost and never came out again. I could still feel the sting of Tata's hand on my cheek. He'd never so much as raised his hand to me before. But this, I deserved.

I walked into the house like a zombie. Night of the living dead. That's what I felt like. I didn't bother to take my clothes off. I didn't care if the noose strangled me. I'd already hanged myself at the dance.

I curled into a ball on top of my sheet. In my nostrils lingered a smell stronger than that of smoked pig, more fragrant than Nana's orchid lei or Daphne's plumeria blossom. I could still smell the musty odor of incense. I tried not to think about Tomas or Daphne. Or what vile, evil things happened to Nana nearly thirty years ago. For the first time I understood what drove Tatan to chase that Japanese man with a machete. Thinking about what happened to my nana filled me with such pain I was sure my mind snapped and I had become as crazy as my tatan.

CHAPTER 14

REGRETS

JANUARY 14–15, 1972

Seto had hid in his cave long after he'd heard gunfire. He cowered in silence. He did not go above ground that night. He stayed burrowed below the next day, contemplating whether to go out at nightfall. He thought he would starve to death if he did not go hunting one more night. But if he did die, who would know? He was already buried.

Finally, he sat up upon his mat. What did he have to fear? Death? Was he not already dead in many ways? He was dead to his family. He was dead to the world. He had more contact with spirits and ghosts and crawling things beneath the earth than he did with man or beast above his grave.

Seto wished he had *sake* to dull his senses and warm his belly. Root tea would have to suffice. The root tea tasted like mud, but he needed something warm to flow down his throat and through his body, and even out in piss, just to prove he still lived.

He crawled to the compartment of hell where it was hottest—his stove. He rubbed two sticks together until his hands hurt. A spark caught dried leaves on fire. Seto blew his breath of life onto the fire until it danced yellow and blue beyond the smoke. Seto touched his finger to the flame until it seared. He jerked his finger back. Hot pain let him know he could still feel, therefore he must be alive.

He inhaled the musty smoke and coughed, further proof he breathed. Could a ghost cough, or start a fire, or feel heat?

"Ha! Aiee, hee, ha!" Seto made belly sounds that forced his breath out in spurts. It was his way of saying, *I live! I live!*

After drinking root tea and blowing out the fire, Seto pulled on his clothes, climbed out of his pit, and pushed through the hatch. Once in the jungle with his feet planted on a mossy floor, Seto breathed deeply, as deeply as the first god who sprang from a reed, to smell damp leaves and earthy scents.

He patted his suit. *"I am a man, not a worm that crawls up naked from underground."*

His voice creaked like branches bent by wind. The sound was not muffled as when he spoke underground. Seto opened his rusty jaw and made "ooOOoo" sounds. He howled like a dog.

"Let them find me," he whispered, and walked toward the river. For what would they do to him that he had not already done to himself?

What could his father do to him even if Isamu came home disgraced?

Long ago he hid like a coward. Tomorrow he may hide again. But for tonight he needed to feel alive.

CHAPTER 15

BLOOD BROTHERS

JANUARY 15–16, 1972

I lay on my bed exhausted. I don't know which stung worse, my cheek Tata'd slapped or my pride. Yeah, I deserved it. No one would probably speak to me for the rest of my life. Especially not my best buddy. And I could forget about Daphne ever liking me after I humiliated her in front of everybody. I might as well become a monk.

Talk about being unworthy. The priest must have been reading my thoughts when I took Communion and saw my mind was plenty confused. God must have been checking out my heart, and knew it was a heart of darkness. No, He probably didn't even want me, certainly not for the priesthood.

My mind kept rehashing last night at fiesta. What had the old biddies said? It was as if geckos with their *chirp-chirp-chirping* mocked the gossiping *maga'hagas*:

Shamed, eh? *Chirp chirp.*

Poor Roselina . . . *Chirp, chir-chirp.*

Where Sammy came from . . . *Chirp, chir-chirp, chirp, chirp.*

. . . soiled by those nasty Japanese fellas . . .

Soiled.

Shamed, eh?

I must have dozed off, but not long enough before Nana woke me for Sunday Mass. I pushed my head deeper into the pillow. I didn't feel like going to Mass ever again.

"Ah, Nana, can't I skip? Doesn't last night count?" I grabbed the corners of my pillow and flopped it over my face.

"Kiko." Nana sat on the side of my bed and tugged at the pillow. "Do you feel like talking about last night?"

I flipped onto my stomach and pulled the pillow tighter over my head.

"Maybe not now, but later, eh?" she prodded. "You hurt your friend's feelings plenty bad."

After she left I threw the pillow on the floor and bounded for the bathroom. Talk? To Nana? About rape? No way! Not then, not ever.

I showered and started to dress in my clothes from the night before. Blood and food stained my white shirt so I shoved it under my bed with my torn jams.

I leafed through my closet for something—anything—to wear. Not that I cared if I showed up in shorts, a T-shirt, and zoris. After all, the monks wear sandals and who knows what else under those robes. But I didn't want to catch grief from Nana, especially not today. There wasn't much hanging in my closet, except Sammy's clothes. I'd never worn his clothes. But just this once—I'd wash them, and even iron them if I had to, and hang them back up.

I pulled out a pair of tan khakis and put them on. The pants grazed above my ankles like high waders. How could I have grown taller than Sammy and not realized it? I threw on a pale green shirt. I had to unbutton the sleeves and roll the cuffs. I couldn't get the top buttoned either so I left it undone and pushed the knot of my skinny black tie up, hoping Nana wouldn't notice.

I hurried to breakfast, famished from not having eaten much at fiesta.

Tatan slumped in his chair, sullen and in a stupor.

"What are we doing with him?" I pointed my fork at Tatan.

"Kiko," Nana said. "Don't talk like he's not here."

Tata said, "Taking him with us, like always."

"Hey, you with us today?" I said to Tatan, who only stared and stayed mute.

"Is he with us today?" I asked my parents. Nana sighed. Tata grunted.

"Fine," I said. "Don't talk about it. Don't talk about anyt'ing. Don't talk about how he runs naked in front of my friends. Or tells family secrets. Let's definitely not talk about how he humiliates Nana in public. Nooo, let's not talk about not'ing when it comes to Tatan. 'Cause then we might have to do somet'ing about him besides make Kiko babysit."

"I warned you," Tata roared and pounded the table with his fist. "Don't disrespect your elders!"

I threw my fork down so hard it bounced. I jumped up and knocked my chair backward. My knee bumped under the table, spilling orange juice and coffee. "What are you going to do? Hit me again?" I kicked the chair out of my way and slammed the screen door. I heard a chair scrape back, probably Tata's, then Nana say, "Leave him be."

Bobo danced on his back paws and scratched my bruised knee. I shoved Bobo down and off the stoop. Bobo landed with a yelp. I stormed down the road to walk all the way to church. I didn't care if I got there in time for the final "amen" or not.

I was relieved when my parents' Datsun, with Tatan in the back seat, chugged past me. Then Daphne's parents drove on by without stopping. It was just as well, Daphne would probably never speak to me again. I kicked a rock down the road until my black church shoes were covered in red dirt.

I'd walked a good ways before a car crawled to a stop. Tomas's tata hollered out his rolled-down window, "Hop in," like it was an order instead of an option. I opened the back door and climbed in beside Tomas.

Embarrassed, I looked out the side window. "T'anks."

"No problem," Rudy Tanaka said.

Tomas's nana made small talk. "How are you today? Nice day for a walk. Sorry we're running late for church."

Why should they be sorry? I was the one who had a lot to be sorry about. Only how could I explain without letting anyone know about Nana? Unless, they already knew. Maybe everyone knew.

I stared out the window and said nothing.

The Tanakas's car swayed with every curve, jostling me off-balance in the seat. As it rounded the last turn, I couldn't stand the rift I'd caused between Tomas and me anymore.

"Sorry," I mumbled.

"What?"

I looked at my friend. "I said 'sorry.'" I looked at the half-turned heads of Tomas's parents. "Sorry to you, too."

Tomas looked out the window.

"It's a hard t'ing to take," his tata said, "but we know Tatan's been stirring up bad memories so we understand under the circumstances. Apology accepted." His nana smiled.

Just like that. No anger. They understood. Sheesh, I didn't know if I understood. Could I ever get past this? Or was it something that would keep getting thrown up until the day Tatan died? I knew I'd never forgive the faceless, nameless Japanese man who hurt my nana.

The car stopped, and Tomas got out. He didn't say a word as we walked into Mass late.

It felt as if the entire congregation turned and stared when I entered San Miguel Catholic Church. I sat on the back pew with the Tanakas rather than joining my family near the middle.

From where I was sitting, I could see Daphne praying the rosary. She looked so pure with her wispy bangs, round cheeks, full lips mouthing Hail Marys, and smooth tan hands fingering clear plastic beads from her First Communion.

She's about the age Nana would have been during World War II. I found myself figuring math problems the rest of the service. *Nana's forty-three. Her birthday's in April. Liberation was July 1944. That'd have made Nana fifteen at the time. My age. Take Sammy's birthday, January 15, 1945, subtract nine months . . . Tata and Nana didn't get married until after Liberation. If Nana was raped, that would make Sammy my half-brother.*

I opened my eyes and tried to concentrate on Jesus hanging on the crucifix on the back wall. Blood oozed from his head where the crown of thorns pressed into his flesh.

That's what my head feels like.

I didn't want to think anymore. I didn't know which felt ready to explode most, my head or my heart.

After the last "amen" and everyone was piling out of the church, Daphne paused where I sat. Before I could say anything, Missus DeLeon looped her arm around Daphne's waist, said, "Come along," and pulled her out the open wooden doors.

After everyone was gone, Tomas turned toward me and put his arm over the back of the pew. Tears rimmed his eyes. "I'm not mad no more, bro. It just hurts so bad, you coming at me that way and calling me a dirty Jap. You know, I don't even t'ink about being Japanese any more than I t'ink about you being Chamorro. I'm just me. Tomas. And we're like family here. You're like a blood brother to me. But then, you know, this war stuff, it gets us all mixed up." He blinked and a tear brimmed over the edge. Tomas turned his head and wiped his eyes with the back of his hand.

I stared at the walls out of respect for my friend. I didn't look at Tomas again until he sniffled back the rest of his emotion and started talking real fast, like if he didn't get it out he'd choke up and not be able to talk at all. "Like how the Ngs have been here for generations and generations but for a while some people treated them as if they were Commie gooks from North Vietnam. Remember?"

"Yeah, I remember. But not us. We knew Danny Ng since first grade. He's a stand-up guy."

"That's right," Tomas said. "All American, loyal red-white-and-blue like the rest of us. But then Tatan gets this *lytico-bodig* and goes all crazy. And suddenly I'm the enemy. Hey, I shouldn't have danced with Daphne. I hadn't realized how bad you have it for her."

I looked down at my hands. "It wasn't you dancing with her, not really. It's more complicated than that." I turned my head and pretended to study the purple banner with a red cross behind a white lamb. "I can't talk about it." My voice was cracking.

"Is it Tatan? I feel sorry for your family. It's got to be tough. Real tough."

I turned away. It was my turn to wipe under my eyes and sniffle. Did Tomas guess how tough? Did he know? Did everyone know about Nana? Did everyone know Sammy's my half-brother? Did Sammy know Tata's not his father? Am I the only one who didn't know? How could I get past this . . . this knowing?

Tomas reached over and hugged me around the neck. I saw Daphne waiting outside the doorway. "I guess I better apologize to Daphne."

"You better, if you ever want her to talk to you again." Tomas punched my arm. "You really like her, eh?"

"Yeah, I like her a lot." I grinned at Tomas. I felt relieved having said it out loud. "Want to come over for dinner?"

"No pig, eh?"

I wiped my face with my arm. "Eh, man, that was one mean pig Tatan and I fixed last night!"

"You bet, one mean pig. But no leftovers, got it? I t'ink I ate half the porker all by myself," Tomas kidded.

By the time we left the church Daphne had gone. I decided I would call her later. I'd never called a girl before. Except that once when I tried to call Daphne and instead got the cross-eyed lion. But I really needed to make this right with her. Tomas and I climbed in the back of the Datsun with Tatan. Tatan might as well have been a hood ornament the way he stared into space.

Tata looked at me and Tomas in the rearview mirror and said, "Nana's really worried about Tatan. He's been like this all day." He turned to Nana. "Maybe we should take him to Guam Memorial, eh?"

"Not the emergency room." Nana put her hand on Tata's arm. "We'll be there forever and I don't know those doctors. I'll call our family doctor tomorrow. If he's like this in the morning, we'll take him to work with us," she said. Tata looked back at Tatan. Nana's brows scrunched together. "Or I'll drop you off at Sammy's and take him on over to doc right away."

Tomas and I glanced at each other. Poor Tatan. I shook my head.

Nobody said anything the rest of the way home. As Tata drove up the dirt and gravel driveway I saw an air force car parked in front of our house. Bobo was barking and scratching at the navy blue car door, trying to get at the men inside.

Tomas joked, "What now? More bombs? Didn't the navy sweep good enough? They had to send in the air force to finish the job."

"No! Mother of God . . . " Nana screamed.

"Oh, God, no!" Tata cried. He jammed on the gas pedal, spurting up gravel, then slammed on the brakes before Nana jumped out while the Datsun was still moving.

We all scrambled out of the car, except Tatan, who sat catatonic in the back seat.

I yelled, "Bobo come!" Bobo lopped over to me, wagging his tail.

The driver, who was an airman, and an officer stepped out of the Ford.

"Sammy! Sammy!" Nana screamed. Tata held onto Nana as she thrashed and ripped at her hair. "Is he dead? Tell me my baby's not dead!"

CHAPTER 16

WEEPING

JANUARY 16, 1972

Why weep green willow?
 Tears frozen on Winter trees.
 Dew drops of silence.

Seto closed his eyes and lay on his back in his tunnel, reciting bits and pieces of poetry. He could not remember who wrote that haiku. Or did he make it up? He clamped his hands across his shrunken stomach. He needed to feel a human touch, to hear a human voice. The only voices he heard were disembodied voices of those who trampled too close to his cave, or uninvited ghosts.

Seto talked to himself, just to hear a voice, any voice, to break the unbearable silence.

"I am no poet. I have no writing utensils. Yet eyes in my heart see a willow branch from a tree outside Imperial Palace. I went there once— only once—on an errand shortly after I was drafted into Japanese Imperial Army. I believe I delivered a message, or did I drive jeep? No matter. I did not meet Emperor nor was I invited in for green tea. But as I waited outside for official orders, it was stifling in my uniform under August sun. I stole down to lake, unbuttoned my jacket, and sat beneath a willow."

He raised his hand and stroked his fingers around air, imagining it to be the royal willow branch.

"This willow has more strength than I. O, I long to be grafted into that tree and be home again. Yet I am unworthy to hide my shame under

a weeping willow beside lowliest hovel in all of Japan." Seto cried out
and dropped his hand.

*"If I lived in Japan, even at most humblest of abodes, I would be din-
ing on rice and seaweed, koi and bean curds, and sweetest rice cakes."*
He wrapped his arms tightly around his middle. His insides groaned
at the thought of such delicacies he had known but not tasted for
nearly three decades.

Seto rolled onto his side. He ran the back of his hand over his
thin scraggly beard, then smoothed his sparse mustache with his finger and thumb. He could not recall what it felt like to be touched by
another human. He pressed his palms against his cheeks, then bent
his fingers and dabbed the backside of them against his forehead.
His cool fingers revived him—but not one iota as much as the sound
of a voice from a face, and the touch of a hand from another human
being would have resurrected him.

*"If I lived in Japan, even on most modest of means, I would dress
worthy of a tailor who is son of tailors. I would fashion myself clothes
of linen. And I would sew wedding kimonos of finest silk, fresh from
cocoons of silk worms that feasted only on mulberry leaves."*

Seto stretched, rolled over on his back, stretched again, and sat
up. He opened his eyes, then blinked and blinked again to clear the
vision before him.

His voice, the voice that broke the silence of his grave, sounded to
him like crying black gulls circling Japan.

*"Instead I sit here naked in stench of coconut oil and cesspool that
smells worse than odor of burnt whale blubber and chamber pots. But
there I had windows and doors to throw open and air out my house.
I could eat when I hungered and drink, ah, even drink sake, when I
thirsted. In Japan I could take walks and go to mountain to pray and
honor my ancestors. Or do nothing but sit under a tree, any tree, even
Imperial Palace weeping willow tree, if I so desired."*

Seto sat up as straight as he could, considering how much his
spine curved, and the ceiling forced his neck to bow down. His
voice had been shouting. It had become as if not a part of him. As if

disembodied. His voice. *His* voice, as if it belonged to someone else. Only it could not be another's voice, for there was no other person to speak to him. No other human to touch his hand, hug his neck, or kiss his cheek. There was no other. No other voice but his.

And yet, he silenced it for fear of being discovered, not beneath a weeping willow, but weeping beneath the jungle.

CHAPTER 17

M.I.A.

JANUARY 16, 1972

"Not dead, ma'am. Missing In Action."

Tata cradled Nana as she sobbed into his chest. I felt numb and useless. I didn't know what to do.

The way the air force colonel explained it, though Sammy's B-52 was shot down over enemy territory, we should be glad he's listed M.I.A. Yeah, right. Glad.

If he were listed as dead, the colonel said, the military would give up looking for him.

"You see, ma'am," the colonel told Nana. "There's a lot of jungle and mountains and caves . . . Yeah, a lot of secluded caves for him to hide in over there. As soon as it's safe, he'll either come out or we'll go in and find him and bring him home to this here island."

He told Tata, "It could be worse. Your son could be a P.O.W. Those places are hell-holes."

Tata whispered, "Prisoner of War? Our Sammy?"

"But he's not, let me assure you that your son is listed M.I.A. That's Missing In Action. See?" He tapped an ordinary brown clip-board as if it explained everything. "Samuel Christopher Charga-lauf, USAF Captain, M.I.A."

Tatan stared mutely into space as he sat in the back seat of our Datsun.

"Is he all right?" the colonel asked after a while, waving his hand in front of Tatan's face. "Do we need to get paramedics out here to treat the old man for shock?"

"He's sick," I said

Tomas added, "Alzheimer's."

"That explains it," the colonel said.

I guessed the officer and his driver must have had orders not to leave until the families seemed normal enough. *Normal.* I knew our lives would never be the same again. "Uh, t'anks for coming." I extended my hand. "T'anks for telling us about Sammy."

The colonel shook my hand, then Tomas's. He said, "I'm sorry, ma'am," to Nana and patted Tata's shoulder a couple of times. "If you need anything, call the Red Cross. Anytime." The colonel dug in his uniform pocket, pulled out a card, and handed it to me. "Have them call this number."

"Will do, sir." Tomas and I walked him to the navy blue car with the driver leaning against the white air force lettering on the door. The airman snapped to attention and saluted the officer. The colonel saluted back. They got in and drove away.

I jammed my hands in my pockets and fiddled with the Red Cross card. It didn't seem real. Sammy was just away, that's all. Like he'd been away at graduate school in Hawaii, or away in officer training school, then navigator school. But he'd come back. Sammy was probably in Thailand on R&R at the beach flirting with some hot chick. He'd be back to Guam soon. Sammy always came home before, didn't he?

Tomas broke the silence. "Want me go home? Or stay?"

"Your call, man." I looked around the yard as if I was seeing it for the first time. I watched the Ford pull out onto the road, leaving a trail of dust. I surveyed the tool and curing sheds as if they were as foreign as the land mine Tatan had dug up. I ignored Bobo when he nuzzled my hand. I looked toward our field between the cow pasture and boonies. The field where Sammy and I had played countless games of baseball.

Sammy . . . my brother . . . lost . . . My head swirled until I was dizzy from thinking. Sammy, my brother. Tata loves Sammy as much as he loves me. He didn't care where he came from and I shouldn't either. *Sammy's family . . . he's missing . . . and Nana's heartbroken.* My chest felt tight thinking about it.

I stared off into the boonies, trying to imagine my brother hiding in a jungle far away. Was it a jungle like this one? Or more dangerous?

Tomas interrupted my thoughts. "Why don't I get you all lunch."

"I'm not hungry."

"Yeah, but somebody needs to feed Tatan. He don't look so good. I'll be right back. You going to be okay if I leave you alone? You don't look so good either."

"Go ahead. I'll be fine," I lied. Nothing would ever be the same again. My head felt as if I was about to pass out.

Tomas went in our house to call his parents.

"I'll be all right," I said to the empty air, as if saying it would make it so.

Tomas's parents brought fried chicken, sweet potatoes, baked plantains, and taro tips especially for Tatan. No one ate much.

The Tanakas stayed until nightfall. Tomas followed me outside to the field where we played ball. I dropped down onto the pitcher's mound and stared into the boonies.

"You okay, bro?" Tomas asked.

"Yeah. I guess." But I didn't believe it. The war was winding down. Why did Sammy have to go? Why? He could have stayed on Guam and built things. Isn't that what engineers are supposed to do? Not go navigating airplanes over war zones. Wasn't Guam enough for Sammy? Weren't we enough for him? Nana and Tata need him. I need my brother. I wanted him back. It was all I could do not to slam my fist into the ground.

"'Night, then." Tomas started to walk away. He stopped and called back. "See you at school tomorrow?"

I shrugged.

"Call if you don't go." He turned to walk to his parents' car, then hollered back one more time. "Call either way."

That night I had the kind of nightmares I knew I could never tell anyone about. Not ever. The kind of nightmares that if others knew

I had they'd lock me up in the loony bin. Because only sickos would have those kind of nightmares. A guy'd have to be loco to tell anyone he actually thought those things. Even if it was in my sleep and I couldn't help what crazy things ran through my mind.

In this nightmare I saw a woman—sometimes she was my nana, then the face and body would switch to that of Daphne. The woman was half naked. But it wasn't the kind of pleasant dream where a guy wakes up with wet sheets. Instead the half-naked woman cried in pain, writhing to get away. In each dream segment I couldn't stop the rapist. I was pinned down by a man—sometimes he had the face of Tomas, most of the time it was Sammy.

I wanted to hide my eyes and not look. I was ashamed. I wanted to turn it off like a bad TV show. But, being a dream, I had no choice but to watch in horror as the nightmare grew worse. Women struggled and screamed and sobbed. Men became more brutal as they forced the women. I tried to fight. I wanted to punch, strangle, kill the men who hurt my nana and Daphne, the women I knew and loved. It didn't matter if I knew the men. Knew their images to be false images. I hated them. I hated them enough to kill them.

I awoke soaked with sweat and fear and hatred and rage. My body trembled like the volcano that exploded with lava to form Guam. But there were no cooling ocean waters to quench my fire.

CHAPTER 18

M.I.A. IN THE JUNGLE

JANUARY 16, 1972

Seto sat among bamboo stalks, hypnotized by lightning bolts. Flashes of light cast ghastly shadows in the jungle. It conjured ghosts of Privates Yoshi Nakamura and Michi Hayato and memories of the day *Amerikans* drove them into the jungle.

Rumbling thunder took Seto back to that day in 1944 when US tanks had rolled over the mountain crest and pushed them deeper, deeper into hiding.

Rat-a-tat, rat-a-tat . . . Seto and Hayato dove for cover.

"Nakamura! Yoshi Nakamura!" Seto screamed over whistling bombs, followed by *ker-boom* explosions. He ordered Hayato to stay. Seto crawled out from under cover until he found the young private, Yoshi, sprawled on the ground, grasping his bloody leg. He'd been hit.

"Get down!" Seto yelled at Nakamura. A high-pitched whistle, then *ker-boom!* Dirt and rocks exploded into the air. They fell on Seto and Nakamura like hail pounded them from the sky. Seto spit and coughed. His vision a blur, he grabbed Nakamura's arm and threw it over his shoulders. He stood, but hunched, and helped drag the private who hopped on one leg to where Hayato lay with his arms thrown over his head.

"Kyu wosuku," Seto commanded Hayato to help. Hayato did not move. Seto kicked him. *"Kyu wosuku!"* Hayato stood up and put Nakamura's other arm over his shoulder.

They went deeper, deeper into the jungle until the sound of gunfire grew fainter than the chirping, hoof beats, and warthog grunting among the tall trees, dense foliage, strangling vines, and thorny brambles that clawed and ripped at Seto's uniform.

When they reached a river Nakamura begged to sit and soak his leg.

"*No!*" Seto said sternly. He looked around for snipers. Though none could be found, he led the men away from water, not even pausing for a drink.

Back toward the base of the mountain, Seto parted vines to discover a cave in the rock. It was not tall, but deep. It would serve their purpose.

Hayato helped Seto lower Nakamura onto the cold stone floor of the cave. Seto ripped Nakamura's pant leg and tied a strip tightly above the bullet hole. Hayato gagged Nakamura's screams while Seto dug the bullet out of with his knife.

When the bullet was out—a trophy Nakamura kept in his pocket until the day he died—Seto sewed the wound shut with his thinnest needle he kept in a tin.

They had made a pact to stay in the jungle until it was safe to come out.

But it is never safe, Seto thought as he listened to driving rain sweep across the canopy of dense jungle. *There is no such thing as safety. It is an illusion for the deluded.*

CHAPTER 19

LOST

JANUARY 17–23, 1972

All day at school I just went through the motions. My mind was everywhere but on my studies. I didn't even feel like talking to Tomas or Daphne. Not even when she came up to me between classes, touched my hand—it was warm—and said, "Sorry about Sammy," or something like that. I was barely listening. My mind felt as numb as my body. When thinking about Sammy I felt like Simon, my pig. Betrayed. Shot. An empty rotting carcass. But I wasn't dead. Dead pigs don't feel pain.

I tried not to think about where Sammy was or how he felt. When the thoughts crept in, I wanted to collapse in a heap and bawl. But I was at school. And people were whispering enough behind my back. I didn't want their pity. I wanted my brother back. So instead I let anger fill my empty shell. I stomped from class to class like I had a chip on my shoulder, not talking to anyone, just glaring into space as if daring someone to cross me the wrong way.

The second I got off the bus and trudged up our driveway I knew deep in my bones something was wrong. I called for Bobo, but he didn't come. I searched for him, as if playing Kick-the-Can. I found Bobo hiding by the tool shed with his tail tucked under his back legs.

I headed for the house and barely reached the stoop when I heard Tatan cursing a blue streak. I didn't even know Tatan knew half those words. I stood rooted on the stoop, afraid to go in. Tatan blasphemed everything and everyone, including God, Jesus, and *Madre Maria*.

I made a U-turn with my textbooks and headed back to the tool shed to hide out with Bobo. "I know how he feels." I scratched Bobo behind his ears. "I just don't dare say it out loud like he does. I don't have no excuse, like *lytico-bodig*, so I'd be in big trouble if I let all my hurt out like that again." Bobo's tail beat against my leg as if he understood every word.

I cracked the door of the shed enough to let light in so I could see to do my homework. A part of me wished Daphne was sitting beside me, touching my hand again. Maybe she'd explain how to do the math problems that weren't making sense. But then nothing did— make sense, that is. Still, it would be nice to have Daphne there, to hear her voice talk about anything, even math, other than Sammy being shot down in Vietnam.

I stared at a patch of sunlight streaming on the dirt floor. Dust danced in the sunbeam. I thought about another time when Sammy and I had sneaked out behind the shed. Sammy was teaching me to play Mumblety-peg. There was a patch of grass in the sunshine. We sat in the shed's shadow. Sammy showed me how to throw a pocket-knife so it stuck into the grass. I didn't think I was doing too good, but Sammy wouldn't give up on me. After I finally got the knife to stick a few times, he showed me other ways to throw it. He did some cool tricks with that knife.

At the time, a part of me thought how neat it was that Sammy would teach me things my parents said were too dangerous for me to do, like Mumblety-peg. But another part of me had been jealous Sammy owned a pocketknife and got to do things I wasn't allowed to do.

Thinking back, the jealous part of me was dumb. Of course Sammy got to do things I couldn't, like stay up later and go swimming or to the movies with friends. He was a lot older. But I couldn't see that then. I just thought my parents weren't being fair. Like it was dumb of me to be jealous about Tata giving Sammy his knife before my brother left for Vietnam.

Nana slipped into the shed and I pretended I was doing my geometry problems. If she looked at the paper she could see I hadn't gotten much done. Nana gathered her muumuu and held it up out of the red dirt. "What are you doing sitting out here?"

I ran my hand down Bobo's spine. "Not'ing."

"Tatan? You heard him?"

"Couldn't help but. What's with him anyway? I'd get hot sauce on my tongue for even one of those words."

Nana almost laughed. "So you would. I took him to the doctor today."

"Yeah? How'd that go?"

"Doc Blas says Tatan's getting worse."

I didn't know what to say anymore.

"Doc says we'll see peaks and valleys until he bottoms out at the end." Nana bent down to pet Bobo. He rolled over on his back to get a belly rub.

I looked at my nana, trying to read the meaning in her face, but all I could see were dark half moons sunken under her eyes, and sad crinkles around her mouth.

"I don't really understand it myself. Somet'ing about how he'll have good days and bad days."

"Doesn't sound much different than the rest of us." I patted Bobo's belly. "He's just having a bad day, eh?"

The tightness in Nana's face relaxed. "Yeah, guess you're right. We're all having a bad day today. Must be Tatan knows it, too."

"So, did doc give him anyt'ing? You know, medicine to make him more better?"

"Not really. There's not'ing for dementia. Not yet, doc says. But he gave him some pills to help with his moods. That's why he's not so out of it today."

If the situation weren't so serious, I would have laughed out loud. Pills for Tatan's moods! He was certainly in a mood, if that's what it could be called.

"Let's go back in the house," Nana said. "I need to cook fish and fried rice and red beans for supper. Doc Blas says to make sure Tatan eats regularly."

"In a minute. I want to finish my homework."

What I really wanted was to be alone and think about Sammy a little longer. I pitched pebbles into the patch of sunlight, imagining I was playing Mumblety-pegs again. I did that for a while and then remembered what had happened after Sammy showed me how to play the knife game. Nana caught us. She yelled at Sammy, said I was going to get hurt bad and it'd be his fault.

"You grounded!" Nana had shouted at Sammy.

He laughed one big "Ha!" and said, "I'm too old to ground."

Nana looked as if she was ready to swat Sammy on the butt. But then she ordered, "Go to your room!"

Sammy did as she said. I didn't know if he was griping under his breath or laughing. I followed him to our bedroom. I'd figured if Sammy was grounded then I wanted to be grounded, too. Just so I got to hang out with my big brother.

I got up off the ground and brushed the dirt off the seat of my pants. I picked up my geometry book and took it to our room—Sammy's and mine.

The next day Tata threatened to lock Tatan outside for the night so they could get some sleep. But Nana wouldn't hear of it.

Tatan cursed continually for four days. "Worse than a movie house," Tata said. Finally Nana shouted, "Enough already! I'm taking him back to the doctor."

Tata didn't argue with her, even though it meant he'd have to run the shop all by himself and cost plenty mullah for doctor bills and medicine. "I was saving that money to fix your kitchen."

Nana patted his arm. "It can wait." She kissed his cheek.

By Thursday night Tatan seemed to have slipped back into his stupor, but by Friday he rose before the sun, banging pots and pans, wanting to cook breakfast. I believe he would have, too, if he only knew where Nana hid the stove knobs.

By Sunday I could tell Tatan's mood medicine kicked in plenty good.

"Tatan's riding high on that 'purple mushroom' he's taking, eh?" I kidded Nana.

"Don't you be making fun of Tatan." She shook a spatula at me. "Besides, doc says his good moods wouldn't last, so enjoy it now before he takes another turn for the worse."

Tata convinced her they had to skip Mass and work at the Quonset Hut. "Bills are piled high and inventory's backed up."

I actually wanted to stock shelves to help out. But knew I was helping more by being at home looking out for Tatan. Nana didn't need to fret much about him, what with all the worrying she was doing about Sammy.

"We'll miss Mass just this once," Tata said. "Or we'll start going Saturday night at the basilica in Agana on our way home from work."

That was fine with me. I didn't feel like going to Mass lately. Except I missed seeing Daphne, watching her say the rosary. I did get to see her on Friday nights when I went to Catechism. But the closer it got to Confirmation, I felt more and more . . . dirty. No, what did the priest call it? Unworthy. That must be what I felt. I couldn't explain it any other way.

By one o'clock I guessed Tomas must be home from church so I called and asked him over for a game of baseball.

"You sure you want me over there, bro? How's Tatan?"

"Sure, I'm sure," I said, snaking the phone cord around my hand. "Tatan's fine. In fact, he's great! Doc's got him high on some mood elevator. He's buzzing better than if he chewed betel nut sliced with lime."

"*Humph.* Like you'd know."

Tomas arrived with his bat and a big basket of food his nana insisted he bring. "So you boys don't eat everyt'ing at Roselina's and make that poor woman have to cook tonight," Tomas said, imitating Missus Tanaka's voice.

Tatan cracked jokes that would have been funny if they weren't so old I'd heard them millions of times. Tomas laughed though. Bobo even picked up on Tatan's "elevated" mood and scampered around like a young pup.

"Come on, let's get Tatan to play ball with us." I smacked Sammy's baseball into my glove. "That way we can keep him happy and out of trouble."

We had the best game going since forever. I reveled in the cool ocean breeze and light shower that misted me down after working up a sweat running bases.

Tatan and Bobo were a sight. Tatan bunted and Bobo chased balls in the outfield. It wasn't real clear whose team they were on—mine or Tomas's—but I didn't care. I couldn't remember the last time we'd had such fun together.

"And it's a bunt to the infield," Tomas said in his sportscaster's voice, as Tatan trotted to first base.

"You know, bunts aren't so bad. Better to stay out of the boonies that way."

"What?" Tomas said. "You afraid of power-hitter Tanaka?"

"Afraid? Me? No way, man. Pla-a-a-y ball!" I wound up a pitch. I looked left to see Tatan standing between first and second. I pretended to throw the ball at Tatan to get him out. Which was a joke since no one but Bobo was there to retrieve the ball.

Tatan ran back to first. "Ha. Ha! Can't get me. I'm safe!" he shouted.

Tomas called, "Bobo! Go deep!" Bobo barked and skipped in circles in the infield.

I wound up my arm again. I pitched square across the plate.

Tomas swung the bat from above shoulder to chest. *Cra-ack.* He followed through.

The ball sped a line drive past the pitcher's mound and straight for the river. I dove to keep from getting hit. Bobo's nose followed its path, and he took off running. Tatan slow-ran around the bases, making sure he touched every one.

I got up, dusted myself off, and ran toward the boonies.

"And it's a home run!" Tomas said, sportscaster style.

Tatan rounded second base.

I chased Bobo into the boonies. I searched near the river.

No ball.

Bobo must have picked up a scent because he followed a trail upstream.

I followed deeper into the underbrush, knowing Tomas hit this one farther than ever before. Muffled by the distance and boonies, Tomas's voice was calling for me. I paused only long enough to yell back, "It's Sammy's ball! I have to find Sammy's ball!"

It sounded as if Tomas said, "He'll understand. Come back. We'll get another one."

I didn't want another ball. No other ball would do. I didn't want a hundred new balls. I wanted this baseball. Sammy gave me it to me. What if I never saw him again and this was the last thing he gave me?

Deeper and deeper into the dense boonies, Bobo and I searched. I looked for traces of mashed down plants, or any sign that a ball had whizzed through the foliage. It didn't help that Bobo did his own mashing and breaking of ferns and limbs.

I passed a banyan tree. I decided it would be a waste of daylight to climb it. I passed where I'd seen the dead snake. All that sat there was a rock. I passed the place where I remembered a man's footprint had been. I looked again to see if my eyes, or the *taotaomona* spirits, had played tricks on me. Maybe. There was no snake, no footprint today.

Bobo veered away from the river and barked at something he pawed at in the dirt. Maybe he found Sammy's baseball.

"Fetch it, Bobo!" I whistled. "Bring it here, boy!"

Maybe the ball was stuck. Or it wasn't Sammy's ball after all. Maybe he'd cornered an animal instead.

Either way, I needed to get Bobo and head back. Daylight was gone. I'd have to wait until tomorrow to search again.

I'll look every day until I find it, Sammy. Every day until you come home.

"Bobo." My dog glanced up for only a second then resumed scratching.

I trampled through the underbrush to some bamboo stalks seemingly set apart in a tiny forestland of their own. I looked down to see what Bobo was scratching at under fallen bamboo leaves scattered on the jungle floor.

"What the . . . no animal made this." I reached for the bamboo mat tied together with coarse rope. I stopped. Better not. I left it alone.

"Bobo, no!" I hissed, trying to keep my voice low. "Let's get out of here."

I grabbed Bobo by the scruff of his neck and pulled him away from the handmade mat. Bobo kept his head up, and sniffed and bobbed his neck from side to side, as I dragged him away from the inhabited area. Bobo reared up on hind legs, growled, and bared his teeth. I'd never seen him like this before.

I spun around and saw something. What was it? A man? He looked . . . wild . . . dirty . . . hunched. A stench reeked through the air, not like anything I'd smelled before.

Bobo lunged and broke from my grasp. "Bobo, no," I called. "Come!"

I watched thrashing in the impenetrable brush. Bobo's barking turned to yelping, then snarling, then high-pitched yip, yip-yips.

I plunged into the thicket, not caring that the underbrush cut my legs. "Bobo!" I shouted. "Bobo!"

I found Bobo lying in the brush, blood soaking his belly. I rushed to see if he was still alive. Bobo panted hard in between deep throaty moans. I stood up and looked in every direction. What monster would do this to my dog? I couldn't imagine anyone I knew on Guam, no matter how mean, hurting a dog. But this wasn't an animal attack. My blood boiled and I wanted to punch someone or something. I twisted in circles, searching, searching, for who did this.

No one. No sign, except for Bobo bleeding.

"Let's get you home, Bobo." I cradled my dog in my arms and carried him out of the brambles and brush, past palms, banyan, and breadfruit trees, along the Talofofo tributary until we were well into the clearing where Tomas and Tatan waited for us in the dark.

"How'd this happen?" Tomas called and ran toward me.

"Bobo's hurt. Let's get him back to the house and see how bad." I wasn't sure I wanted to tell about the wild man in the boonies until I sorted things out for myself.

Tomas rubbed Bobo behind his ears, which drooped down. He whimpered.

"Got your ball?" Tatan asked.

I shook my head "no," then nuzzled my face into Bobo's neck.

No one talked as we walked back to the house. I was relieved my parents weren't home yet. I laid Bobo on the kitchen floor and asked Tomas to fetch rags. Tatan got a drink of water and went into the living room and turned on the TV.

I carefully dabbed reddish-brown blood from Bobo's yellow fur. "It's not that Tatan doesn't care about Bobo."

"It's his sickness, maybe the medicine, eh?" Tomas said, more as a question.

I told myself if I concentrated on Bobo, I could push the anger down inside somewhere, deal with it later. Bobo needed me more at that moment. Tomas kept staring toward the living room, looking at Tatan watching TV, as if nothing happened. I cleared my throat. "I don't even know if he understands about Sammy . . . being lost and all."

Tomas chucked his chin. I went back to washing Bobo with a rag, being as gentle as I could not to hurt him.

Bobo licked his ribs. Once the blood was cleaned from his fur, Tomas and I inspected a deep gash under his ribcage.

"What would have caused that?" Tomas asked. "Looks like it's punctured."

I didn't say anything. I wondered if I hadn't gotten there in time, would the man have killed Bobo?

I knew then for sure, beyond a shadow of a doubt, that what I had seen was not a *taotaomona* spirit playing tricks on me.

I had seen, with my own eyes, a real, live man.

The gaunt, stooped-shouldered walking skeleton with a sunken face and hollow, dark eyes had to be a Japanese straggler stalking the boonies not far from our house.

I shook thinking about it. What if I'd been all alone, or Bobo, or Tatan? What would the straggler have done to any one of us?

I went to the bathroom to find some medicine. I poured peroxide into Bobo's wound. He yelped and nipped at his sore. I spread thick ointment on the cut, then wrapped and tied my gray T-shirt around Bobo to stop the bleeding.

"Let's get Bobo to the shed," I told Tomas. "Nana will pitch a fit if she finds him in the house."

I carried Bobo and Tomas took rags and old towels I didn't think Nana would miss. There was another reason I wanted Bobo in the shed. I didn't want Tata and Nana to ask questions. Not tonight. I had to think this through. I was so angry I couldn't stop shaking. My heart was still thumping, as if I had run a marathon around the island.

While Tomas helped me fix a bed of towels and rags for Bobo, headlights shone through the tool shed window. I grabbed Tomas's arm. "Don't tell anyone what happened!"

Tomas looked like a deer stunned by car lights.

I relaxed my grip. "I'll tell them later."

Tomas nodded.

"I better get home before I'm grounded for being out too late." Tomas jumped up and opened the shed door.

"No!" I practically shouted. "Wait for my tata to drive you home."

He cocked one shoulder and gave me a *what's-the-big-deal?* look, then started out the door.

I bolted toward our car, waved my arms, and shouted, "Tata! Tata! Take Tomas home. He shouldn't be out after dark."

Tomas gave me a strange look, as if I'd lost more than a baseball in the boonies. "Eh? I'm no baby. I see myself home after dark lots."

"No! Tata, drive him home. Please! I'll go with you."

Nana climbed out of the passenger seat. She looked tired. Tata stuck his head out of the car window. "No problem. Come on, Tomas. I'll drive you."

Nana patted Tomas's cheek. "Tell your nana *si yu'us ma'ase* for me."

"Will do, ma'am. I'll t'ank her for you," he said, then headed for the car.

I was halfway in the car when I hollered to Nana, "Lock the doors. We'll be back shortly."

Tata and Tomas looked at each other and scrunched their eyebrows. No one on Guam locked doors. How could I explain this?

On the way home from Tomas's house, Tata asked me, "Son, is there somet'ing you want to tell me?"

I wanted to talk to my tata about so many things. Words had dammed up inside of me for too long and I was angry and scared and confused. But instead of spilling about the straggler in the boonies who stabbed Bobo, I blurted out, "I know I look like Tihu Tony, but who does Sammy take after?"

Tata's head jerked toward me and he glared. "Who you t'ink he takes after?" Tata exploded like a volcano. "Me! Me!" He thumped his chest like a drum. "I'm his tata!"

My heartbeat speeded up so fast I thought it was going to explode like a grenade, if my head didn't first. I wished I could take back my words.

"Don't you ever question again who Sammy's father is. Not to me, not to Sammy, and especially . . . " Spit flew. " . . . don't you dare ever say anyt'ing to your nana. She's been through enough hell without you giving her more grief."

Grief. That's what I was giving them. That's why I couldn't tell them anything. I buried my big mouth into my fist and leaned my splitting headache against the cool side window.

Tata drove up the dirt roadway and parked. I waited until Tata stomped into the house before I peeked through the shed door at Bobo. He was asleep. Once in the house I locked the outside doors and went straight to bed. But instead of stripping down to my underwear I laid still beneath my sheet, fully dressed in shorts and T-shirt.

What if I had to get up in a hurry?

Thoughts ran through my brain faster than a school of *manahac* in spawning season.

How long had the straggler been there?

What was under that bamboo mat staked to the ground?

What would the man do now that he knew I knew about his location?

Did he know where I lived?

Those were the questions that bothered me first. Curiosity questions. Fear questions. Self-preservation questions.

Then came the "what if" questions. Questions of conscience.

What if I told?

Who could I tell? *Humph.* See if I'd ever talk to Tata again.

What if Tatan found out? . . . He'd kill that Japanese soldier.

. . . *What if I killed the soldier first?*

Who would know? I could get Tatan's machete and gun, and sneak into the boonies without anyone looking. I knew where he was hiding. It would be easy. I'd find the Japanese soldier, surprise him, kill him, and drag his body deeper into the jungle. No one would know.

If someone found the body later, no one would know it was me who killed him.

No one would know who the man was. Probably not even in Japan. If his family wasn't dead already, surely they'd given up hope. He'd been missing forever. There was probably a clipboard somewhere in Japan, maybe at the emperor's palace, or in some dusty filing cabinet. But there it was, an old brown clipboard with a rusted clasp holding together a yellowed paper that had this soldier's name under M.I.A.—Missing In Action—or whatever they called it in Japanese.

No one would care. Surely his family had all given up on him ever being alive or coming home.

CHAPTER 20

STRAGGLER

JANUARY 23, 1972

Seto cowered in his cave. His hands clutched a hard mud-covered object.

Seto had been delighted earlier to catch a coconut crab. A crab big enough for a feast! Big enough to stop the nip, nip, nipping of hunger in his belly. *Hai,* Seto was truly delighted. Carefully holding his knife and crab away from his bare flesh, Seto practically skipped like a school-boy back to the bamboo thicket that concealed his tunnel.

Something whizzed past him. Seto threw his arms over his head and ducked to the ground. He listened for gunfire. Instead he heard scratching on the jungle floor. His crab! It'd scurried away.

Seto retrieved his knife and searched beneath leaves, branches, brambles for the coconut crab. A round object, much smaller than the crab that got away, caught his eye. He squinted closer. *Ah, could it be? This far into the jungle?* Seto bent and picked up the muddy thing. A different type of delight quickened within his chest. A warm feeling covered his heart and spread to his face. His eyes rained tears. A piece of home nestled in his hands. He clutched a baseball.

He took a step toward the river to wash off mud. Tonight luck smiled upon him. Maybe she would give him another crab. He would look among trees and leaves.

Something much bigger than a crab rustled behind him. A distant voice called, "Bobo!"

No time to waste. Seto rushed toward his cave.

Too late. A wild animal growled. A boy yelled, "Bobo, no!"

A golden dog lunged through brush. His teeth threatened to rip Seto's throat. Or at least he thought the dog might do so. He'd seen rabid dogs in China attack and tear a man apart.

Seto stabbed the dog and ripped his knife downward like gutting a deer. But he had not pushed the knife in deep enough. Only enough to wound the animal.

Quick. Quick. Boy is coming, his thoughts screamed.

Seto ran. He'd circled back to his cave once he was sure the boy had left.

As he cowered in his cave his heart beat loud against his chest, and muscles in his arm strained against his hand squeezing the baseball. He was afraid to let go. He had already lost his dinner. He did not want to lose his memory of childhood.

Aiee. The boy had seen him. It was the native boy Seto did not kill before. If only the dog had not barked.

Why did Seto not kill the dog and drag it back to his lair before the boy came for it?

I am as slow and weak as the snails I eat, Seto lamented, hammering the baseball against his mouth. Dog would have filled his belly plenty.

Would the native boy and old man and golden dog with big teeth be waiting to kill or capture me? Seto wondered as he rubbed mud off the baseball. *I should have finished them off, then they would not be a threat.*

Seto tried to spit on the ball where the mud had dried. His mouth was too dry, and his tongue like sand.

Should I leave my home?

He rubbed his thumb over red threads. Such nice, tight stitches. Seto thought of his father laboring over his sewing machine. Had his father ever admired stitches on a baseball? Seto wished he could ask his father. But knew his father must be dead. Seto sighed.

I am too old to move.

He rolled the ball between his hands.

Will men come hunt me now? Or can I chance going up to hunt my supper? I will starve if I gather no food tonight.

Seto slammed the baseball to the ground.

I am starving already.

He buried his head beneath his arms. The dirty white ball mocked him. He was no longer imprisoned in his father's tailor shop. Yet Seto still could not go outdoors and play baseball.

He tucked the ball into a box with his sewing kit. He wiped his eyes, then crept to a broken coconut shell and examined the empty brown husk. Alas, he had scraped out the last white meat for bait and did not fetch another coconut in his haste to escape watching eyes.

Seto crawled to his stove to sip final drops of river water he had boiled. He found the pan empty. *Evaporated, every drop.*

He had no choice but to go up and search for food and bring back water.

Later. When Sun sleeps behind horizon and Moon shines her face above trees. At twilight I go up . . . for a moment . . . these tired bones will try once more to quench my thirst and feed this hungry flesh.

Seto picked at shredded pago bark to weave more cloth.

If I think too much, I go mad.

CHAPTER 21

NIGHT CRAWLERS

JANUARY 23, 1972

In the dead of night, I slipped out of bed. I pulled on blue jeans and a black long-sleeved knit shirt with an aqua surfboard on back, and "Hang Loose" printed on the front. Only "Hang Loose" was the last thing I planned to do. I dug out black socks and black leather church shoes from my closet, but didn't put them on until I reached the tool shed.

I unlocked the front door and creaked opened the screen, pausing only long enough to hear if anyone woke up. All clear, I tiptoed to the shed, shushing Bobo as I opened the door.

Blood had seeped through the T-shirt around Bobo. I carefully unwrapped it, and winced when I tore it away from my dog's fur that was matted with brown dried blood. I dabbed more salve onto the wound, ripped the T-shirt into strips, and tied the three cleanest cloths around him.

I stroked Bobo's back, hugged his neck, then got up and searched for a weapon. I stretched to reach behind the oil can perched on the shelf above my head. I fingered the cold metal of the gun Tatan used to shoot Simon.

No, not the gun. Someone might hear.

I lifted Tatan's machete from two pegs, slicing air as if sharpening a barber's razor on a leather strap.

I couldn't imagine hacking a man to death. Too messy.

My eyes raced over tools mounted on the wall—claw hammer, plumber's wrench, screwdrivers . . .

Nothing . . . not there . . . Ah! I knew what to use.

I checked out the wheelbarrow where I'd laid the tools to dry after washing blood off them.

Seemed right. I picked up the knife I slit Simon's throat with.

I fetched a rope and wound the cord, thumb to elbow, then hung it over my shoulder.

I rubbed Bobo behind the ears and led him back to his bed of rags. "Stay here boy," I whispered hoarsely. "I've got business to take care of. No one's going to hurt you, or Nana, again." Bobo clapped his tail against the dirt floor as if he approved of what I was about to do.

I slipped out the door, latched it to shut Bobo in, and headed for the boonies.

At the baseball diamond I paused and stared into dense dark foliage. I listened into the darkness, trying to gain courage to press on. All I heard was the lowing of cows. *Moooo, moo.*

I tried to think of Sammy and his baseball in the boonies. It would be no different than running in to find my ball. Or racing into the jungle to rescue Sammy from the enemy. I closed my eyes. Behind closed lids, I conjured up a vision of my nana crying. The tears turned into rain in a jungle where I saw Sammy cowering, scared, crying for help.

I lunged from home plate to thick underbrush without looking back. I walked past mango groves and tangantangan vines to the banyan tree. I listened for *taotaomona* spirits whistling through the leaves, but heard nothing but a mosquito *buzz, buzz* in my ear. I stepped over roots and pressed on past pandanus trees to the thicket of bamboo where Bobo had scratched something manmade.

I crouched behind a palm and cluster of tall ferns and peered into the eerie dark, searching for the Japanese straggler.

Just so the soldier didn't spy me first.

I swatted a mosquito from my ear and listened. Crickets and bullfrogs sang, *Chirp, chirp. Croak. Ribbet. Ribbet. Chirp, chirp. Croak. Riiibbet.*

Cautious . . . curious . . . I struggled with whether or not to lift the bamboo mat and see what lay beneath.

Later. After I'd taken care of him.

With no sign of the straggler near the bamboo grove, I stalked to the marshy reeds. I crouched in weeds and peered up and down the banks of Talofofo, looking for the Japanese soldier.

Everything was still as death; not a soul to be seen, beast or man. My stomach churned. With anxiety? Relief? I wasn't sure which. Maybe he moved elsewhere.

I thought about giving up the hunt and going back home to my safe, comfortable bed when I heard taunting in my head. *Chicken. Buullk, bulk, bulk, bulk. Chicken. The soldiers murdered. They raped. Don't you care? No one will know . . . no one . . .*

I stood, shifted the rope back onto my shoulder, fingered the knife, and walked upstream. I thrashed through underbrush rather than risk being seen on the open banks. I searched in all directions for signs of the soldier.

Slant-eyed devil? Where are you?

Swish, swish, splash.

I halted. I squatted back down in weeds and looked at the river. Ripples circled out on the water.

Probably a dumb old fish.

I started to get up again and head back when just feet ahead of me reeds parted. I sat on my haunches, keeping my gaze on the reeds.

A grimy little figure dressed in coarse shorts and a shirt the color and texture of coconut husks blended with the underbrush like a chameleon. He dipped something into the water and scooped it up again.

My feet inched closer . . . closer . . . until I drew close enough to see the soldier filling a canteen stamped US Army on the side. Close enough to smell the man.

Eeww. Worse than pig poop.

The Japanese soldier pulled up a poorly woven shrimp trap made from split reeds. Empty. I relaxed my grip on the rope. The soldier checked two more traps, all empty. No wonder, they needed mending.

With knuckles swollen like plum seeds, the man thrust into a coconut a crude metal object the shape of a big wooden spoon lashed with a rope to a piece of wood. I'd never seen anything like it before. What'd he have it tied to? The butt end of a rifle?

The straggler twisted the homemade tool and cracked the coconut open. He bent his head back to drink the sweet milk.

Yeah, that's it, rapist. Keep your head back.

I gripped the knife and rope, got down on all fours and crawled slowly, quietly, toward the soldier. If I could get behind him, I could wrap the cord around his skinny neck and slit his throat.

The soldier scraped coconut meat with the metal tool. He put coconut shavings in the traps for bait.

Good. The soldier didn't see me. Just another foot and I could . . . do . . . it. . . . I knew I could. I slit Simon's throat, hadn't I? And Simon was my friend.

The soldier lowered the traps into the river, then moved a few feet over to pull up another trap.

I quit crawling. I didn't want him to see me.

I kept my eyes glued on the soldier's every move. I watched the wisp-of-a-man scrounge for fallen breadfruit. He picked up a rotten one, then dropped it. I tried to imagine this puny walking stick with funny black shocks of hair sticking out in all directions committing vile, evil acts *maga'hagas* whispered about.

This is a Japanese soldier, I thought, psyching myself up to kill him. *One who beat our tatas and raped our nanas. I'm justified in taking his life. I'm justified. He murdered our people. No one will know. No one will care.*

I watched the hunched-over skeleton pluck snails from a tree trunk. He didn't look like a soldier. I wondered what Sammy's eating. Was he finding fresh fruit? Or was he hunting beetles, cockroaches, and rats?

The nearly starved man cupped his hand and chased a frog. The frog hopped away and plopped into the river. The straggler was in such bad shape he couldn't even catch a frog.

It was hard to believe he was once a murderer.

The sickly old man who looked more animal than human lifted a rock and dug out white fleshy grubs to put in his sack.

Maybe he wasn't a rapist.

I rubbed the handle of my knife between my thumb and forefinger. I squinted into the darkening boonies in the direction of my home, then back again at the straggler.

The straggler unbuttoned his shirt and pants, took off his clothes, and quietly lowered himself into the river to bathe. The top of his head above the water's surface looked like the back of a turtle swimming. It reminded me of the stories Tatan told me about the turtle that birthed our island. It was as if I could hear my tatan calling me "Little Turtle."

The dirty soldier lifted his head and looked past me with slanted, fearful eyes. Black marbles, glassy as a doe's, only instead of lids, skin lay over his eyes like the backs of spoons, with an extra fold near the outer corners . . . like Sammy's. Where was Sammy hiding? In a cave? In a jungle? Would some Vietnamese boy find him and kill him? Or have mercy on him?

"Another day," I whispered to the *taotaomonas*.

I slipped back past the marshy reeds. I wove through the dense underbrush, and walked by the bamboo thicket.

Woo. Woo. Wind called me through bamboo like the sounding of a conch shell.

I ventured over to the thicket.

Gong. Gong. One large bamboo shoot drummed against the others.

I looked at the woven mat, then stared in all directions to see if the straggler was coming back.

Probably still searching for food.

I bent down and lifted the mat. Underneath was a hatch like on a submarine, beneath the hatch, a bamboo ladder.

I searched the thicket again for signs the straggler was near.

I'd be quick about it and out before the straggler got back. I lifted the hatch and stole down the creepy hole.

Down two steps, three, four . . .

The air was warm, sluggish, thick.

I'm suffocating. Like I'm sealed shut in a casket.

I strained to look below but couldn't see because it was too dark. I lowered my rope down the shaft but didn't feel it slack up.

Was it a bottomless pit?

I hesitated. Five, six, seven steps more . . .

The stench smelled of burnt coconut oil and death.

I can't breathe! I'm suffocating!

Woo. Woo. Gong. Gong.

Wind scattered leaves on bamboo overhead, sounding like skeleton bones.

Surely *taotaomona* spirits were warning me to get out.

Like a bat spooked out of a cave, I scurried up the bamboo ladder. I stomped the hatch down and tossed on the mat. I rushed to a banyan tree and trembled among its roots.

I'd rather take my chances with *taotaomonas* than go down a shaft so deep and dark even spirits were afraid to haunt.

Scrrrape. Thump. Scrrrape. Thump. Scrrape. Thud.

I hunched down and peeked around the tree. I scaled the roots, then trunk, then branches to peer out toward the bamboo thicket.

The straggler had returned, dragging his burlap sack. Like a skittish deer, he looked in all directions.

The Japanese man peeled back the mat, opened the hatch, and lowered his sack and canteen below.

I shivered, afraid my loud telltale heart would give me away.

I climbed down the banyan and was ready to drop to the ground when the man reappeared and sat on the brink of the pit. He stripped off his filthy burlap clothes, folded them neatly, and descended again into . . .

Hell. That soldier lives in hell.

CHAPTER 22

SURRENDERING

JANUARY 23, 1972

Does he think I did not smell him? I have become like an animal with a keen tracking nose. It must be because I am nearly blind between darkness of my cave and soot from burning coconut oil. But I smelled him. It is just a matter of time before the boy and his dog find me.

Seto sighed deeply and sunk to the floor of his cave. He lay still, as if already dead. What would he do when that day came? He was too tired and weak to fight. Instead, his back bent over like a tailor bends from too many years of sewing in dim light. Maybe it was time to surrender. What would it matter to anyone? Japan was defeated. What happened to the emperor? Is Seto's father even alive? He thought not. Although, his father's ghost never visited him in his cave.

He inhaled deeply, filling his lungs with the smell of burnt coconut oil and mildew from the packed dirt. He coughed in painful spasms until he curled into a ball, gasping for breath.

Maybe it was time to surrender. Seto had already proved he was a coward and could not go the way of the cherry blossoms. His stomach groaned from hunger. At least as a prisoner he would get fed.

Maybe it was time . . . maybe . . .

Seto was too tired to get up and cook the few provisions he had gathered. He was so very, very tired of it all.

CHAPTER 23

MISSING TATAN

JANUARY 24, 1972

I woke up suffocating, strangled in my sheet like a mummy. I felt like crap. I'd even slept in my clothes. I couldn't have dozed off for more than a couple of hours. The alarm clock faced away from me. I was too tired to bother picking it up and checking the time. Then I remembered, and groaned—I had wanted to kill the Japanese soldier.

But I couldn't do it. I couldn't kill that pathetic old man in the boonies.

What if it were Sammy? I wouldn't want someone killing my brother in the Vietnamese jungle, or mountains, or wherever Sammy was hiding as an M.I.A. (It made me feel better to imagine Sammy hiding in a cave beside a river like the Talofofo.)

No matter how much I hated what some soldier did to my nana. No matter how much I hated what happened to Tatan to make him so bitter. I didn't want to become what I hated. I didn't want to live in hell.

I had to tell someone right away about the straggler living in the boonies. But who?

I fought my way out of the sheet, nearly falling on the floor. I sprung up and ran to the kitchen before taking a shower.

Tatan sat at the table drinking coffee and eating an egg and cho-rizo tortilla.

"Where's Tata?"

"*Humph*, that all you got to say to me? No *buenas dias*?" Tatan asked.

Tatan acted like he forgot to take his "purple mushroom."

"*Buenas dias*, Tatan. Now, where's Tata?"

Tatan went back to reading *Ayuda Line*, a question-answer column in the *Pacific Daily News*, and drinking black Kona coffee. He said to no one in particular, "I see they building more hotels on Tumon. What the Japanese couldn't conquer, they buy."

"That's good, Tatan. Means Sammy's Quonset Hut will make more money."

Tatan glared at me.

"More tourists, more sales," I said. No response. I gave up. "Where's Tata and Nana?"

"At work."

"How come?"

"'Cause of all those damn tourists."

I didn't know what to do. Was it safe to leave Tatan home alone? The straggler had a knife, and he'd cut Bobo. Should I skip school? Should I call Tata at work?

I opened a jar, stuck my fingers in, and fished for pickled mango.

"Hurry," Tatan said. "Or you miss the bus."

"I'm t'inking about not going to school today."

Tatan gave me the *atan baba*. "You go. Or else."

I knew better than to challenge Tatan with "or else, what?"

"Tatan, if I go to school today, will you promise me somet'ing?"

Tatan scrunched, then lifted his eyebrows. "If? . . . promise somet'ing?"

"Promise me you won't go in the boonies today."

"Or else?" Tatan said. "What?"

"Just promise me. No boonies today," I pleaded.

Tatan furrowed his eyebrows.

I flicked my eyebrows up. "Or else . . . I no go to school today."

Tatan stood, pointed his finger toward the door and roared, "You go! 'Cause I say so!"

I grabbed my books and slipped on my zoris by the door. I creaked open the screen door just wide enough to squeeze out without letting

Bobo wiggle in. I must've been so out of it the night before that I didn't lock the shed back up. Bobo had worked the rags I'd wrapped him in down on his rump and looked like he was doing a crazy hula. I dumped dog food into Bobo's dish and fixed the rag back around his cut. That'd have to do until I came home after school. I craned my neck toward Tatan and hollered into the kitchen, "Promise. No boonies. Please."

Tatan was already buried back in his newspaper. He mumbled, "Deal," then raised his head, pounded his fist on the table, and yelled, "Go to school!"

I ran down the dirt lane. It was the first time I could recall Bobo didn't follow me. I was concerned he wouldn't be a very good watchdog anymore either.

At school I was bursting to tell Tomas and Daphne. But they couldn't do any more good than I could. In class I got yelled at for not paying attention. Oh, I was paying attention all right—to the clock. The hands clicked so slowly I daydreamed of smashing the glass to hurry them along. What if Tatan didn't listen to me and went into the boonies? Why hadn't I told Tata or someone when I first suspected there might be a Japanese solider living behind our house? How could I have been so blind to the signs someone was there? I had to get home and check on Tatan.

When school was finally out and the bus crawled home, I jumped down three steps off the bus and raced up the lane to my house. Bobo had worked the rags loose again and was licking his wound. I took the bloody rags off while rubbing Bobo's head and telling him to leave his cut alone. I'd go through the bathroom cabinet for supplies to fix him up. But first I needed to check on Tatan.

"Tatan, I'm home," I called as I bounded up the steps. "Tatan, you here?" I kicked my zoris off and dropped my books on the kitchen table.

No Tatan.

Please . . . no. He promised!

I looked in the living room. Tatan wasn't watching TV. The bathroom door was open so I went in and got salve, gauze, and tape. Then I looked in Tatan's bedroom.

Whew! He's napping. Good deal. I'd just have to keep an eye on him until Tata got home. Tata'd know what to do once I told him about the straggler.

After I tended to Bobo I fetched a carton of milk, fresh coconut, leftover red rice, tortillas, and fish from the refrigerator. That should hold me until Nana got home and fixed supper. A couple of times I picked up the receiver to call Daphne. I needed someone to talk to, I was so antsy. Once I almost dialed her number. But each time I put the phone down and told myself, *Later.* This was not a good time for a first call. I was too keyed up and jittery.

I felt too exhausted and wired to concentrate on homework, so I took my snack in the living room to eat in front of *The Partridge Family.* They were pretty goofy *haoles,* not like any family I knew. But the singing wasn't half bad. I turned the volume low so as not to wake Tatan.

Several hours later Tata and Nana still weren't home. I called Sammy's Quonset Hut. "Nana? Is Tata there? When you coming home?"

"Oh, Kiko," Nana said. "I'm sorry. I should've called. We're going to be late."

"How late?"

"I don't know. We're doing inventory. We have to get this done tonight. You and Tatan okay?"

She sounded dog-tired. "Yeah. Kay-o. We're fine. Tatan's sleeping. I'm getting ready to do homework."

"That's my good boy. Go ahead and fix somet'ing to eat."

"Nana?"

"Yeah?"

"Can I talk to Tata?"

"He can't talk now, Kiko. He's ringing up customers . . . Wait . . . Eh? Yeah? . . . Kiko, I have to help him find somet'ing. You know your tata, he gets impatient when he doesn't understand Japanese. He says I'm more better at it." Nana forced out a little laugh. "We'll be home soon, Son. I love you. 'Bye."

I stood listening to the dial tone. *I love you too,* I wanted to say, but hadn't since I was a little boy. Bobo barked from outside somewhere. I hung up the phone and went to the screen door. I didn't see anyone, but Bobo didn't bark for nothing.

Tatan'd been napping a long time. Maybe I'd better check on him.

Tatan wasn't in his room. Not again! What he'd do? Sneak out while I was watching TV?

I ran to the tool shed. The busted lock hung loose on the hinge and the door swung open. Bobo couldn't have opened it that wide, so I went inside and checked for what was missing.

Tatan's machete.

I reached up on the shelf and behind the oil can for the gun. I wrapped my fingers around the muzzle.

Should I take it with me? I lifted the axe-patterned butt end. *Nah. Not a good plan.*

I grabbed the sickle instead and ran to the boonies. Bobo joined me at the edge, sniffing wildly. The sun lingered above the horizon. The moon sat high above the coconut fronds. An eerie haze settled over the jungle.

"Tatan! Tatan!" I shouted.

Bobo's nose led him in a serpentine path.

"Tatan! Tatan!"

We reached the river. Something moved by the banks. It was hunched over. No. . . . There were two . . . It was . . .

. . . deer. How could I mistake deer drinking from the river for humans? I felt so stupid. Either my eyes or the *taotaomona* spirits were playing tricks on me.

I sickled over to the bank. Bobo lapped water from the river.

The straggler was out there. I'd seen him! He had a knife. He'd hurt Bobo already. He could hurt Tatan. I had to find him. I had to.

My heart pounded like drums. I was breathing so shallow I felt as if I was suffocating again.

Bobo ran ahead, but I kept calling him back, fearing Bobo might get knifed like the other day, only worse.

I followed the river, veering off toward the bamboo thicket. As I rounded the banyan tree, my heart was divided. I looked off into the boonies, searching for signs of the pitiful, wild-eyed straggler. But foremost on my mind was Tatan. Where was he? More importantly, was he safe?

If anything bad happened to Tatan, it'd be my fault. I hadn't told anyone soon enough about the straggler. What if it was too late and he'd killed Tatan?

CHAPTER 24

M.I.A. FOUND

JANUARY 24, 1972

Once above ground, Seto invoked his vow of silence.

He stood ankle-deep in water by the riverbank, hidden in thick reeds. *I must hurry and check shrimp traps. If my stomach had not protested I would not have chanced coming up tonight. It is too risky since native boy knows I exist.*

Seto scooped water into a pot. He longed to quench his thirst but dared not drink without boiling it first. *After all, my sanitation system drains into this river, and never can tell what else dirties water. It would not be dignified to die of dysentery.*

He almost chuckled, but froze at the sound of a voice calling, "Tatan!"

Is it that boy with his golden dog calling old man?

Seto very, very slowly squatted down in reeds. He plunged his hands into water and sloshed out two shrimp traps. *I will take them to my cave, set and bait them later when danger has passed.*

From on top of the hill, the boy called out again, "Tatan! Tatan!"

"An-ton-e-o? An-ton-e-o? . . . " a voice hollered from the jungle below the sword grass. He called more words Seto could not understand. The boy got very excitable and jumped up and down when he heard the voice from the jungle. The boy and his golden dog ran back down the knoll.

Seto began to stand up. He stopped and knelt.

The voice is clearer. He is too close. Seto crouched back down, rested on his haunches, and waited.

He listened to the swoosh, swoosh of footsteps trampling through dense underbrush.

Stand very still, Seto told himself. *I dare not run. I barely breathe; fear has caught my breath away. If I could only spy out . . . a little . . .* Seto thrust his face forward, trying to peer through reeds.

Ah, he gasped.

A husky old Chamorro man held a machete, like a samurai sword, high above Seto's neck. He did not twitch a muscle. One downward swing and he would be beheaded.

"Do not let me die here!" Seto cried to Kannon for mercy.

CHAPTER 25

CAPTURE

JANUARY 24, 1972

Tatan lifted his machete above the Japanese soldier's head.

"You raped my Rosie!" Tatan cried, trembling.

"Nooo . . . !" I screamed and ran, never taking my eyes off them. "Tatan, stop!"

The shriveled old soldier dropped whatever it was he was holding and put his hands together in front of him. He bowed his head slowly to the ground. The whole time Tatan shook. Tears flooded his eyes and fell down his cheeks like a waterfall.

When I reached them I stopped dead an arm's length from Tatan. I held out my hand, like that day on the beach. The Japanese straggler had his eyes squeezed shut. How could he stay bowed to the ground like that? Was he praying? Or waiting to be executed? No! This man wants to live or he wouldn't have hidden for so long.

"Tatan. Give me the machete. You don't want to do this. You are not a murderer."

The soldier opened his eyes and looked at me, as if pleading for his life.

Tatan raised the machete. The soldier winced and cowered lower to the ground. Tatan cried out, "My Rosie! What have you done to my Rosie?" Hysterical wailing rose like tsunami waves out of Tatan. In all my years I'd never seen him in such gut-wrenching pain.

"Tatan," I said, trying to keep my voice calm but firm. I moved my hand toward them. The soldier flinched. I realized I was still holding the sickle. I tossed it behind me as if throwing a Frisbee.

Bobo growled and bared his teeth at the straggler. I wouldn't blame Bobo if he bit the man. I know I'd wanted to, after what he'd done to my dog. But I didn't want Tatan to behead him.

"Tatan, give me the machete. This man is innocent."

"He raped my Rosie!" Tatan stood up straight, raising the machete above his head. Snot ran from his nose but he made no attempt to wipe it.

"No!" I held my hand steady, but inside I was jellyfish. "Look at him Tatan! Look at him!" I pointed to the old soldier bowing on the ground. "The war is over. This man is defeated. He's a walking skeleton. For Christ's sake, don't do this!" My eyes were blurry from sweat and tears.

I blinked to clear my vision and saw the machete lowering. I lunged, which was a really stupid thing to do. But I couldn't live with myself if Tatan killed this man.

Tatan slashed the machete downward. It swooshed to the ground, narrowly missing the soldier. The Japanese man collapsed to the ground and curled into a fetal ball. Tatan dropped to his knees and buried his head in his hands, sobbing uncontrollably.

Breath heaved out of me. I reached down and picked up the machete, then sat down in exhaustion. "God, have mercy on us all," I muttered as I wiped tears and sweat.

I don't know how long we all stayed like that on the ground—not long enough to rest, for sure—when Tatan stood up. I scrambled up, too, and shouted, "Get up!" to the Japanese soldier. I didn't know what to do with him. But I wasn't going to go through this hell again. Tatan bawled behind his hands like a shamed child. I patted his back. "It's all right. It's going to be all right."

The soldier slowly stood, bowed to me, then straightened as much as he could with his hunched back, and said, *"Dai-jobu. Dai-jobu."* I wasn't sure what he'd just said, but there didn't seem to be any fear or anger in his voice. All I could think about was that I needed to get Tatan home safely. I wondered what the word "home" was in

Japanese. I know that's where Sammy would want to go if someone found him in the jungles of Vietnam.

I put my arm around Tatan's shoulder and pointed to Bobo, still baring his teeth and growling at the soldier.

"Let's take Bobo home. It's over. It's all over."

Tatan grabbed Bobo by the scruff of the neck and pulled him until Bobo gave up guarding the soldier. But Tatan looked confused about which way to go, so I nudged the straggler and led him away from Talofofo River, through underbrush, and past the bamboo grove. When we got to the bamboo mat, Bobo sniffed wildly. Confusion still clouded Tatan's face.

I called, "Bobo! Home!"

The straggler looked straight ahead, as if he didn't know anything about what was under that mat. He turned his back on his underground tunnel and we marched on through the path I'd cleared earlier toward the pasture.

I led them past the cow pasture, and beside the baseball field, being careful to keep the machete by my leg. I didn't want to seem menacing. The straggler was coming along peaceably. I was glad for that. But I wasn't sure what to do with him once we got home.

The man stumbled. He lay on the ground. When he didn't get up Tatan and I sat down beside him. Tatan searched through a pouch. He pulled out a fruit bat. The straggler shook his head, so Tatan put the dead bat back into his pouch.

"Come." I stood and motioned for the straggler to get up. Tatan stood, but not the Japanese man.

He pointed to the pouch, then pointed to his mouth, motioning he wanted something else to eat.

Tatan placed his huge hands palms up, fingers spread, showing he had no more to give. I pointed toward the field beyond the boonies. I was careful not to raise the machete. I didn't want to spook him any more than he might already be scared.

He got up and went with us. When we walked past the pig pen, the Japanese straggler said in broken English, "Made sick. No more eat pig."

I looked at him. Was he trying to smile, as if he'd made a joke? Tatan lumbered past us both and took Bobo into the house.

The straggler hesitated at our doorway. For a moment I thought he was going to bolt. I carefully set the machete down on the stoop, then opened the door wider.

"Wa-ter?" the straggler asked hoarsely in halting, broken English.

I pointed to the kitchen sink, visible from the doorway. "Water."

The Japanese soldier stepped over the threshold and into our house. I couldn't read his face—astonishment, yet fear? I shook my head. I couldn't imagine. He'd been hidden in the jungle longer than I'd been alive.

Tatan and Bobo weren't anywhere to be seen. It was probably for the better. I didn't care if Bobo was drinking out of the toilet and Tatan was taking a nap. Just so they were both in the house and safe. I'd check on them later. At the moment I had to figure out what to do with this very dirty, very hungry, and very, very lost World War II Japanese soldier stinking up our kitchen. Man, would I have some explaining to do when Nana and Tata got home.

I opened the refrigerator and dug out fish and rice and set it on the table. I poured a glass of water from the faucet and a cup of cold coffee from a pot left on the counter since breakfast.

The man devoured the fish. Next he shoveled rice into his mouth with his fingers. Food belched up his pipes, but he swallowed it down again, and held up his empty bowl and plate.

"*Arigato,*" he said. I knew that word, *thank you*, in Japanese. He added in English, "More."

I gave him the rest of our supper and figured Nana would understand. While the soldier was wolfing down fish and rice in between gulps of water and coffee, I sneaked to the phone in the living room and dialed, as quickly and quietly as possible, the police.

I turned my back to the doorway—and soldier—cupped my hand around the receiver, and whispered, "Get to Ferdinand Chargalauf's house right away. A Japanese straggler is here."

I quietly settled the receiver on its cradle. I wanted desperately to call my tata, but couldn't risk leaving the soldier alone.

I rushed back to the kitchen and hunted for more food. I didn't want him to get sick from eating too much. I didn't want to have to clean up vomit. But I couldn't think of how else to keep him there. For the second time in two nights I knew what was meant by "sweating bullets," because that was what it felt like I was doing. My heart pounded out of my chest. I was so scared this would all end badly.

Just when it seemed we were totally out of food and I was debating whether to give him dog food to eat, I was relieved to hear a vehicle pull up outside. When I looked out the window I saw it was a jeep.

I went over to the straggler and squatted down to be on an equal plane with him. I didn't want to startle him, and was afraid having the authorities come to take him away would freak him out.

"Uh . . . " I wished I knew Japanese at that moment more than anything. It was too late to call Tomas. But even if Tomas was there, I don't think he could begin to express all the things I wanted to say to this man.

"Men . . . nice men, are here to help you." I smiled, hoping he could tell I was being friendly.

There was a knock at the door and the straggler jumped and looked around. I checked behind me and saw Tatan standing in the doorway to the living room.

"It's the police chief," I said, not taking my eyes off of the straggler. "Come in!" I called, but not too loudly.

The door opened slowly and the straggler pushed back the chair. "It's all right," I said calmly, steadying myself with the table as I slowly stood up. *Don't panic*, I kept telling myself in my head. The last thing I needed was mayhem in Nana's kitchen. I was going to have a hard enough time explaining everything that happened tonight, including why I gave away all our food.

It was a good thing I knew the police chief. After the night of the bomb, nothing should have surprised him. But as soon as he saw the World War II Japanese solider in our kitchen, he cried out, "Mary, Mother of God!" and then was speechless for a while.

By the time they got the straggler to the jeep I was really feeling sorry for him. As scared as I'd been, he had to be terrified. I bet he was sweating bullets, too, and a lot more. There was a reason he had hidden in the boonies so long, and now he was going to have to face whatever drove him there in the first place.

The solider hesitated getting into the jeep, but he didn't put up a fight or anything. Finally he bowed to the police chief and climbed into the jeep.

"Son, you and your tatan better come along," Chief Ada said. "I suspect the military brass is going to have a lot of questions for you back at the station."

I helped Tatan into the front seat of the jeep, then went back and found Bobo shut in the bathroom, where Tatan had probably put him. Sure enough, there was water all over the floor where Bobo had slurped from the toilet. I locked Bobo in the shed, then locked the house and climbed into the back of the jeep.

"Wait," I said as the driver started to pull away from our house. "I need to call my parents or leave them a note."

"You can call from the station," Chief Ada said.

Great. I just hoped when the police called my parents they wouldn't think Tatan and I had been arrested.

CHAPTER 26

SETO'S PLIGHT

JANUARY 24–25, 1972

Seto was not tied to the chair at the chief's office. But still he could not run away.

Aiee, here come men in uniforms. So many uniforms. I do not recognize . . . Ah, hai. There, I see US for United States . . . Amerikans have come to arrest me. This is what I have feared for twenty-eight years. I am prisoner.

Flash!

Ai-ee! My eyes. So bright to my eyes. Seto covered his eyes after camera bulbs blinded him.

Many men, some in uniform, circled around him. Even if he could run, where would he go? Did he want to live like a hunted animal again? It would be worse this time because the men knew he existed.

He sat exhausted. Too exhausted to talk anymore. He let the native boy do all the talking. He accepted he was a prisoner. Too exhausted to resist.

A Japanese man came through the door, stood in front of Seto, and bowed. *"I am Japanese Consul James Shintaku,"* he said in Japanese.

James, so strange, why would a Japanese man have a Christian name? Christians are foreign devils.

The man named James pointed to the chief and called him mayor, and introduced two native policemen. He pointed to a native dressed in military uniform, and said he was an army lieutenant. Him, Seto was afraid of most. Another military man snapped a camera that blinded Seto.

He couldn't remember all of the names and titles—too many men in the chief's office. But there was one woman—it was nice to see a woman, even if she did wear a blue uniform dress with a badge on her shoulder—about whom Japanese Consul Shintaku said, *"A Red Cross lady is here to see that you are treated fairly."* Seto noticed he did not say "prisoner." Who could he trust more? Japanese Consul with Christian name or Red Cross lady, or no one? Except maybe the baseball boy who brought him out of the jungle and fed him fish and rice. The boy kept the old man from beheading him, and the golden dog from biting him.

"Name? Rank? Squadron? Commander served under?" Consul James Shintaku interpreted army lieutenant's questions.

For the first time since he had been brought into the mayor's office by the old man with the machete and the boy with the golden dog, Seto stood to his feet. He straightened up as best as his feeble spine could, put his arms to his side in a soldier's stance, and faced forward. *"Isamu Seto, Corporal, Thirty-Eighth Infantry Division, Supply Unit at Talofofo Camp, Commander . . . "* He faltered. His commander and comrades must all be dead.

Consul Shintaku urged him to sit down again. The Red Cross lady brought him water in a paper cup. The boy who no longer had the dog, and the crazy old man who no longer held the machete, were standing in the back of the crowd. No one was smiling. They all looked so serious, as if he was in trouble.

"Who are you? Where have you been living? What did you eat? How did you survive?" The consul interpreted a policeman's questions.

Questions. So many questions. It is no use. I will tell them. I will tell them all they want to know. I am their prisoner. Japan lost the war. I have brought shame to my name and my family, as my father knew I would. I am tired. So very tired. And afraid. There is nothing worse they can do to me than the hardships I have suffered all these years living alone underground like a scared rat. I will tell all.

Seto told his tale of war and loss and hiding, but still the men did not seem to understand what he endured to survive. He told his story. He showed his pants he made. If they would only let him go back to his underground home he would show them the suit he had tailored. If he could go back, he would return the boy's baseball since he had given him fish and rice to eat.

Seto convinced them he was indeed a soldier of Japan's Imperial Army who did not surrender. He was a tailor who survived the jungles of Guam for twenty-eight years. The US Army lieutenant, policemen, mayor, cameraman, and Red Cross lady looked at each other, shook their heads, and wondered out loud, "Could other soldiers be hiding?"

A man and a woman—it must have been the baseball boy's parents—rushed in through the door crying, "Kiko! Tatan!" After a bit of commotion, the boy and old man left with them. The boy raised his hand to Seto, as if he wanted to say something, but it had to wait. Seto was sorry to see the boy leave, but not the old man. The soldier had seen that crazed look before, the one he saw in the old man's eyes when he'd held the machete. It's the look of a man haunted by memories of atrocities better left forgotten. Atrocities one cannot forgive.

After a very long interrogation, Seto was led outside to a white square truck. They put him in the back and made him lay down on a bed.

Where they take me? Do I go to prison? What is this vehicle with flashing red lights and piercing air raid siren? I am afraid. So afraid.

Seto peered out a rear window and watched the vehicle he was in race up roads. When it finally stopped, and the back doors opened, Seto was met by polite applause.

Who are these people? These many people? Seto wondered as a nurse in a white uniform dress and hat escorted him down metal steps. *Why, they are Japanese. Who are they? And why they dressed in Western clothes? Where are their kimonos, obis, and slippers? Is this a trick? I do not understand.*

When he asked the consul in Japanese, the consul told him news had leaked out that a Japanese straggler had been brought out of the jungle and taken to Guam Memorial Hospital. The consul said there were many Japanese businessmen from the airlines, hotels, and shipping companies who live on Guam to support the tourist industry.

"They wish to see with their own eyes the soldier who stayed true to the emperor long after they themselves had been told he was not a god but a defeated man," Consul Shintaku said.

"The emperor? Of course he is a god. Who would suggest such blasphemy?" Seto said.

The Japanese community clapped politely. *"Hurry and get well,"* a few called faintly in Japanese as he shuffled through two gray doors that swung open in the middle.

A nurse sat him down on a green wobbly chair balanced between bicycle wheels. He rubbed the fabric with his fingers. It was coarse, but not as coarse as hemp or the clothes he had woven in the jungle. The fibers were so closely knit he could not imagine what wondrous loom had made this cloth. *It must be strong to hold my weight.*

The nurse with the crisp white hat, and nylons—why, they had no seams up the back!—and shoes, pushed him to a ceramic tile room with a Western toilet stool and above-ground tub. The woman asked him something in English and when he did not respond, she began to take his clothes off, even though he grasped the brown trousers tightly in his fists. He was used to being naked. When he grew up in Japan they bathed together—men, women, and children—in one great bathhouse.

There was no shame in nakedness. Yet it had been a lifetime ago since he had bathed with anyone other than shrimp and fish and frogs. So when the woman rubbed a cloth over his body and scrubbed his neck and ears and face, he wished this once not to be touched and found himself embarrassed, an emotion he did not know he possessed. She dressed him in a gown slit open in back. He was grateful when she handed him a pale blue kimono—though thin and cotton, a cloth inferior to silk—to cover himself. She called it a bathrobe.

After the bath, and he did not stink as much, doctors and nurses poked and prodded, observed and pricked his body.

Too many people. Too much light. Needles should be used for sewing, not stabbing me. I wish to be left alone.

Seto raised his arm, bent it at the elbow and squeezed his bicep between his fingers and thumb. "See? I am good, no?" he said in English.

The doctors nodded their heads and murmured. *"A little malnourished."* The Japanese consul translated. *"You are amazingly healthy."*

That night, Seto did not sleep. On top of the bean-green sheets tucked tight over the hard, high bed he lay on his side, curled in a ball, and watched the door for intruders. The nurses came in often, shoved a glass stick in his mouth, and clamped a black cloth around his arm, then squeezed a rubber ball like how a snake wraps itself around a mouse and squeezes it to death before swallowing it whole.

The next day, a young lady in a red-and-white-striped apron over her white dress brought in much food on a tray. At the very smell of food, Seto's stomach rolled and gurgled. She lifted the lid and revealed slices of pig fat slabbed on the plate. No wonder his belly threatened to throw up what he had eaten the day before. He ate one egg instead.

A nurse wheeled Seto down many halls to face new interrogators—*Amerikan* reporters.

Questions. Did I see strange airplanes? Did I know war was over? Did I know Japan lost? Why did I hide?

So many questions. What did I eat? Where was I born? Was I married?

They make my head spin.

A reporter asked, "What will you do when you go back to Japan?"

Consul Shintaku interpreted.

Go to Japan? Is it possible? Would Amerikans really let me go? Go home to Motherland? Japan?

The consul repeated the question.

"I . . . I will take back bones of dead friends and bury them in a mountain . . . I will pray for dead Japanese soldiers."

The *Amerikans* wanted to know where these bones were, and who were the friends he spoke of. Seto told them everything. He had nothing left to keep secret.

The questions kept coming. "Have you seen television?"

"I heard they have one at college in Japan."

"Oh, you must mean motion pictures."

"Do you know about the atomic bomb?"

Seto could not pronounce the word even after Consul said it a second time. Consul tried to explain, how it had been dropped on Hiroshima and Nagasaki, utterly destroying everything for miles around.

"I do not understand," Seto said, then paused as if trying to comprehend. *"Was it a Japanese bomb?"*

A reporter said, and Consul interpreted, "No, an American bomb. They used it to end the war faster."

The interrogators droned on and on, like planes Seto heard from his cave beneath the bamboo thicket.

He grew weak under the weight of heavy questions and lights and cameras. He grew weary under the weight of newfound knowledge.

"Did you know . . . ?" reporters asked. "Did you know . . . ?"

"What would you like now?" one asked.

"Something salty to eat," Seto said, hoping his wish would be granted and the press conference would end.

Finally, it did. However, a Japanese businessman taping the interviews made one more request, *"Ah, ah. Arigato, say one more word. Everyone in Japan is surprised and is waiting for you. One word, arigato."*

"Dai-jobu," Seto said. *"Dai-jobu."* He couldn't imagine life ever being *dai-jobu*. But then, it hadn't been all right for a very long time.

CHAPTER 27

SETO'S LAST DAYS ON GUAM

JANUARY 26–FEBRUARY 3, 1972

"Did you read about the Japanese soldier?" I waved Wednesday's newspaper over the breakfast table as if shooing flies.

"Did you see my picture in the paper with the straggler I brought out of the boonies? My name's in the paper! I found him. Honest." I crossed my heart. "All 'cause Tatan got lost."

I'd told them the story a hundred times since I turned the straggler over to authorities two days ago. I loved how my story made Nana and Tata laugh. I'd missed hearing them laugh, especially since Sammy went M.I.A. Nana kissed the top of my head and whispered, "We're proud of you, Son."

Tatan didn't laugh, though. "Don't you go telling that, boy! You're a liar! Never been lost a day in my life."

Tata and Nana stifled their laughter. But I knew by the way Tata's eyebrows twitched and Nana's eyes danced my parents were pleased with me.

I couldn't wait to take the paper to school. After I had gotten home from the police station I'd called Tomas and Daphne. Boy, was she surprised to hear from me! I was so wired, though, that it wasn't hard to talk to her at all. In some ways it was easier than talking to her in person. The best part was that Daphne said she forgave me for being such a jerk the night of Fiesta. She said she could tell I'd been under a lot of pressure lately. Man, was that an understatement.

"So," I asked my parents, "what scoop Officer Perez giving out?"

"Well," Nana said as she scrambled eggs to mix with leftover rice and beans for breakfast, "hear tell a plane-load of Japanese journalists are flying in today."

"Yeah," Tata added, "along with some old war buddies of Seto's. Hear tell he plenty scared and the authorities are having trouble convincing the old soldier it's all right to go back to Japan."

"Darn shooting, that old Nip ought to be scared," Tatan said. "Enough of us war prisoners would like to sneak into his hospital room and fill him full of lead. That'd teach him."

I was tired of hearing Tatan talk that way about the Japanese. I was ready to go to school for a change. I folded the newspaper under my arm, grabbed my transistor radio, and shoved it in my pocket. Tomas and I listened to it as we rode to and from school by holding it against the bus window to get reception. We listened to KUAM for news of the straggler every chance we got. Even some teachers turned radios on low in their classrooms. When news updates came on, they stopped teaching to let us learn history firsthand. It was neat, really, to think I helped make history. I wondered if my name would be in the Guam history book someday.

By Thursday, the third day after Seto had been captured, Tatan and Bobo were pacing at the bus stop after school. Bobo's cut had been healing nicely. Nana had said I'd make a good medic, the way I cleaned it up and put salve on it.

Seeing Tatan acting so agitated, I started worrying again. Tomas got off the bus with me.

"Tatan, what's wrong?" I asked.

"Damn Japanese. Whole lot of them. All dressed like you and me . . . like civilians."

I looked back at Tomas and shrugged to see if he was okay with Tatan mouthing off about the Japanese again.

Tomas grinned and tilted his chin skyward as if to signal, *I'm with you, bro.*

I placed my hand on Tatan's arm, hoping to calm him down. "Tell me, Tatan. Where are the Japanese civilians and what are they doing?"

Tatan stopped pacing and jerked his head toward Tomas. "He's not one of them. Too young."

"That's right. Tomas is our friend. Remember his tata, Rudy Tanaka? Eh? He was one of the good guys on our side during the war."

Tatan looked at me as if I'd lost my mind. "Don't get smart with me, boy. I know Tanaka. I got to show you those damn Japanese tromping t'rough our boonies. What they doing back there? Stealing my bats?"

Tomas and I followed Tatan and Bobo to the opening by the baseball diamond. It didn't take long until we reached where the underbrush was trampled down.

"Bet a lot of people been snooping around Seto's cave," Tomas said.

"Yeah, probably all those Japanese reporters who flew in yesterday," I said.

"That's what I been saying," Tatan said. "Bunch of Japanese where they don't belong."

In the bamboo patch, there was a yellow taped-off area and Guam policeman standing guard. When we approached, the policeman yelled, "Hey! Stop! No one's allowed here without authorization."

Tatan went up to the officer and tapped his finger on his chest. "You're the one on my land, Sonny. I been hunting and fishing and gathering food from these parts since before you were born."

I touched Tatan's elbow. "Come on, Tatan. He's just doing his job. Let's go home."

Tomas mouthed to the officer, "Sorry," as we all turned to go. The officer shrugged.

When we got to my house, Tomas and I read the newspaper account. "It says here," Tomas read, while I peered over his shoulder, "that two war buddies brought a tape recording of relatives' voices who are still alive in Japan. Seto tried to answer them back when they spoke."

"Imagine that," I said, "he doesn't even know what a tape recorder is. Wonder what else he doesn't know about."

"Damn t'ing," Tatan said. "Probably made in Japan. What they couldn't conquer, they make."

I held my breath and rolled my eyes. I wanted to cover my ears. I was so damn tired of hearing my tatan bad-mouth Japanese people and Japan. But I realized Tatan would never change. Still, it was embarrassing hearing him talk like that, especially in front of my best buddy.

Tomas acted as if he hadn't heard Tatan. "There's the telephone, and, of course, TV." He folded the newspaper and laid it on the kitchen table. "I know, how about skateboards . . . what else?"

I tried to think of new inventions Seto wouldn't have known about since he holed away nearly thirty years ago. "I got it. Bikinis! Seto'd still think Bikini's an atoll in the Pacific."

We burst out laughing.

Tatan scowled. "What's so funny? You two not laughing at me, are you? Eh? Better not be."

*

Seto did not understand why he could not sleep since he came to the hospital. He had a comfortable mattress under a roof in a climate-controlled room. This was the first time since he left home that he did not have to lay on a cold, hard ground in China, or moist, damp soil in the tropics of Guam.

Though guards stood by his door, he had been assured his life was no longer in danger. War buddies, childhood friends, and relatives had flown all the way from Japan to reassure him he would not be jailed or executed. And to convince him it was true, within a week he would board his first airplane and soar back to his homeland, Japan.

Still, he could not sleep.

Even in the safe, warm comfort of a hospital, with pretty nurses, attentive doctors, and policemen outside his room, ghosts haunted him at night.

"Why are you alive and going home?" the phantoms asked in hollow voices to the cadence of their march. Specter soldiers marched, marched, marched by hundreds through his room.

"I have written your names. All of them," Seto told them. *"I will pray to the mountain. I will give obeisance to your names."*

Then appeared Privates Michi Hayato and Yoshi Nakamura. *"Are you going to Japan and leaving us here?"*

"No. No! I will take your bones and bury them in a shrine in the mountains. Why do you haunt me? Have I betrayed you? Do you call me 'coward?'"

Seto waited for the apparition of his mother. She did not come.

Seto dropped his weary body on cold linoleum and curled into a ball.

The next day a distant relative flew in from Japan to visit him.

"Your mother is dead," he said.

Seto showed no emotion. He already knew. Had she not visited him in his cave?

*

Saturday, Daphne's nana dropped her off in our driveway. Missus DeLeon made it clear, "Only for one hour, while I'm at Ladies' Altar Service. And do not go in his house while his parents are not home." She wagged her finger at Daphne at that part of her lecture. Daphne looked very sober at her nana and said, "Yes, ma'am," so I knew no breaking the lion's rules. Or else I'd never be trusted to take Daphne on a real date when I could drive next year.

We took Bobo for a walk in the boonies so I could show Daphne where I found the straggler. Plastic yellow tape still outlined the area around Seto's underground cave entrance.

"Not much action today, eh?" I asked a different policeman guarding the area.

"Nah. All the snoopy reporters went that-a-way looking for some old soldiers' bones." The policemen nodded upstream toward the falls.

"Did you know he was the one who found Seto?" Daphne asked.

I gave the policeman a green mountain apple.

"You don't say?" He bit into the apple. "T'anks," he said with his mouth full.

"Don't suppose I could look down there?" I pointed to the bamboo mat covering Seto's underground cave.

"I'm not supposed to let anyone . . . " The policeman looked in all directions. "But if you don't tell and don't touch anyt'ing. And I mean not'ing! They took one box of stuff out of there the soldier asked for, and the rest they need to inventory."

I wasn't about to wait for him to change his mind. Lickety-split I lifted the mat and motioned for Daphne to climb down first.

She shook her head. "I'll stay up here and watch Bobo. You go ahead."

I started down the bamboo ladder. "Bobo, stay!" I commanded when Bobo looked about ready to plunge down the hole after me. Bobo barked. Daphne kept a firm grip on his collar.

"Five minutes," the policeman warned.

This didn't seem scary at all, I thought. What a difference, climbing down the hole with daylight flooding the shaft and a policeman standing above ground.

But the farther I descended to the bottom, the cooler and damper it got. The walls closed in on me. I was suffocating again, not just from being underground, but from the overwhelming stench. My left foot hit bottom first. I turned, let my eyes adjust to the dimness, and saw Seto's underground cave. I doubled over to make my way into the tunnel.

"Two minutes. Hurry up," the policeman called down the shaft.

I got on my hands and knees and crawled through the cave. I touched the sticky blackened ceiling. "Good t'ing it's supported with bamboo and beams," I said quietly to myself. "Still, wonder how long will it take before it caves in?"

I crawled faster through the tunnel until I reached what looked like a crude campfire spot with stones all around and cooking pot in the center. Stacked to the side, from floor to ceiling, were chopped up bamboo, logs, and coconut husks. I sniffed the pot, which contained something gray and slimy on the bottom. "Yuugg." I gagged back vomit.

I held my breath, only taking quick short breaths when necessary, and crawled to the end of the tunnel where it was hollowed out in a rounded, taller compartment. Light streamed down from a shaft over another, bigger cooking spot. Two tiers of shelves were loaded with old tin pans of assorted sizes, bottles, spoons, a rusted coffee can, and a tea kettle. I touched two plain spoons and ran my finger over a pair of scissors. I wondered if the scissors had been Seto's favorite possession, because the blades were sharpened, probably on a rock.

I knew how he felt. I missed my favorite possession—Sammy's baseball.

I was anxious to get out of the cave, yet curious enough to still linger on my way back through. As I crawled toward the ladder, I paused to look at Seto's clothes neatly folded and stacked beside a mat woven of bamboo leaves. I'd seen *manamkos* weave hats from the long slender leaves. I picked up a case the size of a matchbox and opened the lid. Needles. Made sense, the newspaper article said Seto had been a tailor in Japan and wove and sewed all of his clothes while living in the boonies.

"Boy, get up here. Time's up," the policeman called down.

"Kiko, are you okay?" Daphne's voice echoed down the shaft.

Quickly, I ran my hand over a cloth lying on the mat. Strange, wonder what this was used for? I laid the cloth back down on the mat, scurried to the ladder, and climbed out of the hell-hole as fast as I could.

"Creepy, eh?" the policeman said as soon as my head poked above ground. Bobo licked my face and I pushed him back, anxious to get out of the cave.

"You okay?" Daphne said again.

"Kay-o. Kay-o."

She looked relieved.

"Here, let me help you up." The policeman reached down and clasped my wrist and arm. I grabbed his arm and heave-hoed up top.

I took a deep, long breath, then let it out slowly. "How could anybody live down there? Even for one day?"

"Beats me." The policeman put the bamboo mat back over the hole. "You better get going now."

"T'anks for letting me take a look around."

"Yeah. But no telling, you got me?" The policeman cocked one eye; it twitched.

"Sure, kay-o, we no tell." I petted Bobo's neck and Daphne nodded her head. But before we left I asked the policeman, "Did you see that cloth with all the embroidery? What was that?"

"Weird, huh?" the policeman said. "One of those old military guys who checked out the place said when soldiers in Japan go off to war, people make a thousand stitches on a piece of cloth. They take it with them as a good luck charm. Doesn't look like it worked for him, did it?"

"No, guess not. Doesn't seem he was too lucky having to hide underground all that time."

"If I went off to war, all I'd want is a good gun, bullets, and knife," the policeman said. "I'd make my own luck."

"A knife, eh? Like one of those Swiss Army knives?"

"You betcha," the policeman said. "The best Swiss Army knife money could buy. Never know when it'd come in handy."

Daphne tugged on my T-shirt, signaling we needed to go.

"Well, we best be going," I said. "T'anks again. Which way did you say the reporters went?"

The policeman pointed. I took Bobo's collar from Daphne and pulled him away from the tunnel. We trotted off toward the falls.

We were almost to a clearing when Bobo veered in front of me. I swerved and stumbled over a tree root. Daphne caught me by my arm and steadied me. I slipped my hand in her warm hand. Daphne met my eyes with hers, smiled, and squeezed my hand. The warmth ran up my arm and through my entire body. Even if I wasn't too tongue-tied to say anything, what would I have said to her? I didn't want to spoil the moment. All I could think was, *she likes me! I don't deserve a girl as wonderful as her, but still Daphne likes me!*

We held hands the rest of the way. One part of me wanted this walk to never end. Another part told me that we better hurry up or Missus DeLeon wouldn't let me see Daphne alone again for the rest of my life.

After a long hike through the boonies we came across a crowd of reporters and officials gathered around a cave opening. Bobo slipped through people's legs, but Daphne and I couldn't get through until someone called out, "Whose dog is this? Come and get him out of here!"

"Excuse me, excuse me." I elbowed my way through the crowd, keeping hold of Daphne's hand, to claim Bobo. One policeman restrained a barking, snarling Bobo by the collar. A US soldier held up a plastic bag with human bones and two skulls in it.

Reporters murmured the names Hayato and Nakamura. Evidently Seto told authorities where to look.

"What are you going to do with the bones?" a woman reporter called out.

The soldier, holding the bag of bones, said, "First, we will verify who they were and how they died. Then, if we do find these are the two Japanese soldiers, we've assured Seto and the Japanese consulate we will send the bones to Japan for burial."

I figured we'd seen and heard enough for one day. Not exactly a romantic first date—visiting an underground tunnel, the stench of death, soldiers waving skulls and bones. Still, I wouldn't have traded the walk in the boonies while holding hands with Daphne for anything. The only thing that would have made the day more perfect is if Sammy had been waiting for me at home to tell him all about it.

*

I was getting ready for school Monday morning and found Nana crying while reading the newspaper. Eggs hissed and sizzled and spurted until smoke filled the kitchen. At first I thought it was because Tatan had been acting crazy again so Nana had to take him back to the doctor. But then she crumpled the front page and let the paper drop to the floor.

I waited until my nana was preoccupied scraping burnt eggs into the sink. I picked up the front page, smoothed it out, and scanned headlines to see what upset her.

It couldn't have been the news headline about someone I never heard of defying President Richard Nixon. Couldn't have been about an embargo in British Columbia, wherever that was. Could it possibly have been the smaller right-hand headline?

DEAD COMRADES HAUNT DREAMS OF STRAGGLER

I browsed farther down the page to a small box where I noticed what looked like fingernails had pierced the print:

BOYS DIE IMITATING HERO SETO

The article said four boys from a Japanese elementary school were buried alive. They dug a play cave with a steel pole as they tried to emulate their new hero Isamu Seto.

I looked up at Nana. She stood at the stove crying and fingering her rosary beads.

"Nana?" I wanted to comfort her but didn't know how. "You all right?"

"God help us mothers," she sobbed.

I got up and hugged her until she wiped her eyes, kissed my cheek, then took out more eggs from the refrigerator.

*

Tatan took a turn for the worse Monday night. His speech slurred, his eyes glazed over, and he drooled like a baby cutting teeth.

"Might be the medicine," Nana said. "We saw a different doctor last time, and I heard about drug-drug interaction."

Either that or betel nut, bats, and "purple mushrooms" don't go good together, I thought, but kept my mouth shut.

So, Tuesday morning I skipped school and went to Tumon with my parents to help with Tatan and Sammy's Quonset Hut.

At first I didn't plan to sneak in and see Seto. But once I realized I would be at Guam Memorial Hospital with Nana to take Tatan to the emergency room, I found myself gathering gifts. I scooped sticky rice and tuna Nana brought for lunch into a plastic container. I asked Tata if I could buy some plain wooden chopsticks and dried seaweed from our shop.

"I'll work in exchange."

"Sounds fair," Tata said. "What you need them for?"

"A gift, maybe."

It wasn't until I got to the hospital I realized that seeing Seto wasn't going to be as easy as strolling up to just anybody's room, walking through a door, and saying, "Howzit." There were guards, not to mention reporters and cameramen, and nurses to sneak past.

First I checked out the cafeteria. I'd heard that's where press conferences were held. No one there but people cooking, cleaning, and eating.

Next I went up to the floor where I'd heard rumors Seto was being held. Sure enough, a guard stood at a door by the nurses' station. I decided to hide in the lounge at the end of the hall and think about how to get in to see the old soldier.

When the dietitian delivered lunch, she brought an extra tray for the guard. While he was distracted, I double-timed it down the hall and slipped into Seto's room unnoticed.

Where was Seto? His bed was empty.

The door bumped into me when the dietitian carried in a tray, so I ducked through the open bathroom door and shut it behind me.

"Mister See-toe," the dietitian sang. "Lunch is here."

Silverware rattled on the fiberglass tray as the dietitian set it on the lap table by the bed, then I heard the *swoosh* of the room door shut.

I peeked out from the bathroom. The coast was clear so I walked over to the bed.

Clear broth, Jell-O, milk, and something green and gooey-looking. Maybe Seto was out searching for something better to eat if this was all they were feeding him.

I looked around the room. "Auhh," I caught my breath, startled. In the corner of the room on wadded up sheets lay a skinny, sunken-faced Japanese man with a too-big blue hospital gown wrapped around him. The man grinned, showing several teeth missing.

"I no can sleep in bed," Seto said in English.

"Howzit," I blurted out, then felt like a fool. What should I say? I shifted the container, seaweed, and chopsticks into one hand and extended the other to shake.

Seto pointed to his lunch instead of taking my hand. "You like? You eat. I no like."

I chuckled a little, but not too loud so the guard wouldn't hear. "I brought you lunch." I handed Seto chopsticks and seaweed, and popped the top of the rice and fish containers. The tuna smelled good as it overwhelmed the hospital antiseptic scent.

"Ah! Japanese!" Seto rubbed his stomach, then rose to his knees and bowed at the waist. *"Domo arigato!"* He took the container and shoveled rice in his mouth, then ripped open cellophane and savored every morsel of seaweed.

I gathered my nana's container and walked toward the door. I turned one last time to see the straggler who hid in the boonies for twenty-eight long years—almost twice as long as I'd been alive and for as long as Sammy was old.

"Do you remember me?" I asked Seto.

Seto squinted and cocked his head to the side. "Aaaahh!" Seto said something in Japanese I didn't understand. The soldier held up his forefinger. He got up off the floor and fumbled for a box beneath a steel cart.

He held up a dirty white ball. "Baseball boy." Seto seemed pleased with himself.

I sucked in my breath and took a step forward. *Sammy's baseball!*

Seto stretched his arms and shoulders back as if he was going to hurl the ball across the room. His eyes looked dazed, as if he was seeing something far off. Then he straightened up, relaxed his arms, and extended the ball toward me. "For you."

I took the ball and held it close to my chest. "T'anks." I bowed my head.

"Domo arigato." Seto grinned like a jack-o'-lantern.

*

I begged my parents Wednesday to let me skip school again and to take me to the airport to see Seto off.

"Two days in a row?" Tata teased. "Oh, and I suppose you want I get you an invitation to Governor Camacho's send-off party, eh?"

This brought a laugh from even Tatan, who had acted much more alert since Doctor Blas took away some of his pills.

I grabbed my books and transistor and ran to the bus, not even bothering to feed Bobo or say 'bye.

Second period had barely begun when I looked up and saw my tata standing in the classroom doorway.

"Kiko," my math teacher said. "Looks like your dad needs to see you."

"Get your books, Son," Tata said. "We going to the airport."

On the way to the airport, I said, "Tata, I'm glad you gave Sammy the Swiss Army knife. It's a whole lot more useful than that thousand-stitch cloth Seto had. Never know, that knife may save Sammy's life."

Tata grunted. "Yeah, that's why I gave it to him. I was afraid somet'ing bad might happen over there Sammy wasn't prepared for. You never know. A father worries about his son."

The word "son" lingered in the air between us, Tata behind the wheel, and me hugging the door.

"Kiko, sorry I slapped you."

It was as if Tata's apology took the sting out of my cheek. "Kay-o. T'ings been crazy lately, eh?"

"Crazy. For sure."

"I know it won't happen again." I reached over and patted my tata's hand on the steering wheel. "I forgive you. Forgive me?"

Tata flicked his eyebrows twice, then grinned big. "I have somet'ing for you. Thought I'd give it to you for Confirmation, but you're ready for it now." He reached into his left hip pocket and pulled out an object. Tata kept his hand cupped around it so I couldn't see what it was.

Tata opened his warm hand against my hand. When Tata took his hand away, there lay a bone-handled Swiss Army knife.

"Wow! T'anks, Tata." I dug my thumbnail into the silver notch and pulled out a blade. I switched out another two smaller blades, then a spoon, fork, nail clippers, file, and metal toothpick. "It's a deluxe one all right, like your tatan's." I turned it over in my hand, then handed it back to Tata. "I can't accept it."

"Why not?" Tata didn't take his hands off the steering wheel to take the knife.

Have I committed the unpardonable sin? I asked God in my mind. *I tell you, I wanted to murder that soldier to get even for the man who hurt my nana!*

I laid the knife on the dashboard. "Because I don't deserve it."

Silence hung like a Confessional curtain between us. I turned on the car radio.

Two songs later, Tata turned down the volume. "If we got what we deserved we might not get anyt'ing good in life. I certainly didn't deserve a woman as good as your nana. But she married me anyway."

Tata smiled and I couldn't help but smile back.

Tata picked up the knife off the dashboard and held it out to me. "You earned this more honorably than my tatan did. Have I ever told you how Tatan Bihu Chargalauf got his Swiss Army knife?" Tata shook the knife with each syllable.

"No."

He laughed. "By swapping *tuba* with an American sailor during prohibition in 1899." Tata thrust the knife in front of me. "Take it. It's a gift. You don't have to earn gifts."

For once, I didn't know what to say. I took the knife, ran my thumb over the handle, and stuck it in my pocket. "T'anks." But I didn't have the heart to tell him that I might not go through with Confirmation.

"Now both you and Sammy have knives to pass down to your sons." Tata turned the volume back up and hummed along with the music.

At the airport, Tata and I were like two little fish swimming against the tide in an ocean of people who showed up to see Seto off.

The Japanese man who was escorted up the stairs of a Japan Airlines DC8 barely resembled the straggler I discovered in the boonies. This stooped man was clean-shaven with a fresh, closely cropped haircut, and wore a drab suit.

Did he see me? I wondered. *Nah. Too many people. Too much excitement.*

Seto stepped cautiously up the steel staircase. When he reached the top step, he turned and faced the crowd.

On a whim, I raised two fingers in a victory sign.

Seto raised one hand as if to wave, then halted.

I thought for an instant our eyes met. I bowed my shoulders and head forward, keeping my eyes on the ground.

When I straightened up, Seto bowed a deep bow from the waist forward, then turned and disappeared into the airplane.

The last I heard or read of Seto was that when Japan Airlines touched its Mother soil, Seto stepped out on the gangway, leaned forward, and said in a voice choked with tears, *"Though I am ashamed, I am alive, and have come home again."*

CHAPTER 28

BEYOND THE HORIZON

APRIL 21–22, 1972

"Are you ready?"

I knew Daphne was asking me if I was done setting up chairs so she could finish decorating. Sunday would be the Confirmation ceremony at San Miguel Catholic Church. Our class had spent the entire day preparing the sanctuary and grounds for the fiesta afterward.

But as I looked at her, holding a white satin bow in her hand, waiting to stick it on a chair or table or something, the question haunted me. *Are you ready?*

Am I? Am I ready to go through with Confirmation?

All this time I'd been avoiding talking to our priest about my doubts. I still felt unworthy. Being confirmed into the Church was a big responsibility.

"Go ahead," I told her, opening up the folding chair in my hand. "I'm going to look for the Father." I stepped out from under the shadow of the canopy and into the blinding sunshine. I shaded my eyes with my hand and looked around. Tomas and our buddies were staking tiki torches into the ground. Some girls were filling the torch wells with oil. I didn't see our priest anywhere.

I went into San Miguel. Our church is small compared to most on the island. I poked my head into our classroom. "Father?" No one there. I peeked into his office. "Father?" Not there either.

I walked into the sanctuary, decorated in white satin bows and flowers like a bride waiting for her wedding day. The place was empty.

Toward the front of the church, off to the side in an alcove, is a statue of *Madre Maria*. Someone had lit a votive candle in front of her. I went over and stood above it, watching the light flickering, threatening to go out in the pool of hot wax. I knelt. The candle smelled like a rain-soaked mango. I'd seen my nana light candles many times. I think lately she was lighting them for Sammy.

Thinking of Sammy, I crossed myself and folded my hands. I figured praying was the best way I could mourn my nana's losses—all of her losses, which seemed many on account of the war that stole her innocence, but blessed her with Sammy. And now this other war, the one in Vietnam, that stole her blessing. She certainly had reason to mourn like *Madre Maria* must have done for her own son. No wonder she was known as *Our Lady of Sorrows*.

I prayed a prayer I'd heard my nana pray many times, but never thought about it much before: "O Virgin Mary, no one who ever fled to your protection, asked you for help, or sought your intercession was left unaided. So I come to you, *O Madre Maria*. Before you I kneel, sinful and sorrowful . . . "

A draft, cool on my neck, breathed through the chapel. Darkness covered my closed eyes. I inhaled smoke and heat flushed my forehead. I opened my eyes to dying embers. Quickly I fumbled with the matches. My heart raced, as if this were a bad omen for Sammy. It felt as if Sammy was lost in the dark and scared. He needed his way lit home.

The wick flickered, and stayed lit. My heart quit thumping as I slowed my breath. I continued the prayer with my eyes fixed on the light: "O *Madre* of the Word Incarnate, don't hate my plea. But in your mercy, hear and answer me."

Then I added my plea, which wasn't part of the memorized prayer, but what I really came to beg God for, "Please bring Sammy home alive . . . "

"Kiko?" Daphne's voice. "Oh, I'm sorry. I didn't know . . . "

"Amen." I crossed myself and stood, then lit a second candle.

She turned to leave the sanctuary the way she'd come in, out the back.

"Wait." I hurried toward her. "Did you need something?" I asked when I caught up to her.

"There's a rope that needs cut," Daphne said. "And then we're all done." She smiled at me. I wanted to steal a kiss, but I looked up and saw Missus DeLeon talking to our priest out under the canopy. Daphne showed me the rope that was a tripping hazard.

I pulled my knife out of my pocket—the one my tata had given me. As I cut the rope, the knife reminded me of what Tata had said. None of us are worthy. If we were, then Christ wouldn't have needed to die for us. There was nothing I could do, not pay penance or anything, to earn God's forgiveness. I just had to ask for it.

"It's finished," our priest said, gesturing toward the chairs and tables and flowers and bows. We all marched through the back of the church, gathering our belongings from the classroom before going home.

We walked through the sanctuary and I glanced up at Christ on the cross. *Yeah, it's finished*, I thought.

"Are you ready?" Tomas held the front door open for me.

"Yeah. I am."

"Are you sure? Anyt'ing we've missed?"

"No. Not'ing. Not a t'ing we can do. It's already done." I walked out the door and got into the Tanakas's car to go home.

I hadn't planned to tell my parents that my friends invited me to spend Saturday at the beach. They had enough on their minds with business, Tatan taking a turn for the worse, and them worrying about Sammy being M.I.A.

But when the Tanakas dropped me off Friday after we'd prepared the church for Confirmation, they stopped in for coffee and talked to my parents.

So Saturday morning at breakfast I told my parents that I didn't mind staying home with Tatan instead of going to the beach.

"Don't see no harm in you taking Tatan with you," my tata said. "Do you, Roselina? Tatan's going to be the same no matter where he is. What you t'ink, Rosie?"

Nana stopped spreading cream cheese on bread. She held the butter knife up as if in deep thought, then said, "Your tata's right, Kiko. Might as well take Tatan with you. Just 'cause his *lytico-bodig* is getting worse, Doc Blas says that doesn't mean he isn't fit as a *carabao* physically."

"Are you sure? 'Cause I can stay here with him. Besides, I need to fatten up that new sow tata bought. I want to make sure we have the biggest, most prized pig to slaughter for the fiesta we'll throw when Sammy comes home."

"No, it'll be all right. No sense you missing out on fun with your friends. Tatan's not going to get better just 'cause you stay home," Nana said. "Take a quilt. If he gets tired he can lie down and rest on the beach."

The Tanakas picked up Tatan and me right after my parents left for work. I locked the door. Funny how even little things changed since I found the soldier in the boonies behind our house.

When we got to Talofofo beach, Mister Tanaka opened the trunk and Tomas and I unloaded lunches, a thermos jug of water, and a big stick.

"Here." I handed the stick to Tatan, who was in a stupor. Did he even know it was me, Kiko—his "Little Turtle"? I took his hand and formed it around the walking stick. "I carved this with my knife Tata gave me, then sanded it down and polished it up in shop class." Although Tatan didn't look like he understood what I said, he sighed heavily and leaned on the stick.

"That's cool," Tomas said.

Tomas and I and Tatan started down the steep cliff to Talofofo Bay. "Last day of Spring break," Tomas said.

"Not counting tomorrow, our Confirmation Day." I steadied Tatan by holding his forearm as we slowly stepped from crag to cranny. "Yeah, somet'ing, eh?" Tomas said. "You going to sunrise service here by the bay?"

"Sure, our whole family."

"Ours too. Going to be a long day tomorrow," Tomas said.

I concentrated on guiding Tatan to the bottom safely.

Tomas reached the beach first, then helped me ease Tatan down the final decline. Some of our friends from Confirmation class were already swimming and body surfing. "Hey, bro," Tomas said. "Check out Daphne." He flicked his eyebrows. "Va-va-voom! She's filling out that bikini in all the right places! *Kaboom!*"

I looked out at the ocean. Daphne, wearing a pale pink bikini, ran through the tides with her girlfriends, laughing as they splashed each other.

I glanced back at Tomas, furrowing my eyebrows at him.

"What? What?" Tomas threw both hands in the air. "I thought we were squared away, bro."

"We are. Just don't disrespect them, eh? You wouldn't like it if someone talked about your nana that way."

"Got you, bro. That's cool. No more disrespecting the chi . . . I mean, girls." Tomas smiled and slapped between my shoulder blades.

Daphne turned and ran to me.

I shook out the quilt and it billowed up, then down, like a parachute landing. I put my arm around Daphne's waist and she leaned her head on my shoulder. I studied Tatan's deep-lined face, tanned the color of a coconut shell. I hadn't noticed before that I stood taller than my grandfather.

"Tatan? Want to sit here?"

Tatan looked confused. He stumbled toward the ocean.

"Is he going to be, you know, safe?" Tomas dropped our lunches and thermoses on the quilt.

"I'll keep an eye on him. Go ahead, both of you. I'll be along in a minute, as soon as I know he's all right."

Daphne kissed my cheek and ran with Tomas to join our friends in the surf.

Tatan walked toward the bay and sat down on the black sand. He drew his knees up to his chest. Water lapped back and forth underneath his body as the sun and the moon played tug-of-war with the tides. He gazed far out over the Pacific Ocean.

I squinted into the glare of the sun, trying to see what Tatan stared at beyond the horizon.

Was Sammy hidden away somewhere safe? I looked for a sign that Sammy would come home someday from across the sea like Seto did.

All I saw were rainbows dancing in the spray where the constant waves beat against Guam's shore.

I sat down beside Tatan. The surf surged around us, pulsating in-and-out, in-and-out, hollowing out the sand from under our bodies. Today was a good day. A day of confirmation. I soaked in the warmth of the sun and coolness of the spray. I breathed in the salt air, and watched Daphne and Tomas and my friends play in the ocean. I imagined Sammy there with them, calling to me, "Little Turtle!" I wanted to be strong and steady like the ancient turtle that carried our island on its back. I got up from the black sand and led Tatan to the safety of the dry quilt. Then I turned back toward my friends and ran into the ocean. Sammy was waving to me in the sea foam crests. I dove in and swam against the tide.

Author's Note

Kiko's fictional story began January 3, 1972, when he first learned his nana was raped by a Japanese soldier during World War II. However, the story of Isamu Seto is based on the true-life story of Shoichi Yokoi, the World War II soldier who never surrendered. Yokoi's story began August 5, 1941, when he was drafted into the Japanese Imperial Army.

During World War II, Japan allied with Germany and Italy. Japan invaded China, Southeast Asia, and many Pacific Islands. Shoichi Yokoi, the son of tailors, was drafted into the Third Supply Regiment for temporary duty.

Hours after Japanese pilots attacked Pearl Harbor on December 7, 1941, Japanese forces attacked Guam, which was a United States territorial possession. Three days later, Japan occupied Guam. During the two years and eight months Japanese soldiers occupied Guam, they committed many atrocities against the people. Most of that time, Yokoi was not stationed on Guam. It was not until March 4, 1944, that Yokoi arrived on Guam from Manchuria (China) and was assigned to the supply unit at Talofofo Camp.

The US Marines liberated Guam on July 21, 1944. Germany surrendered May 7, 1945. Japan surrendered September 2, 1945.

But for Yokoi, the war did not end. Why didn't he surrender to the American soldiers and go home to Japan like most soldiers who chose not to commit suicide? I studied news articles written and translated from Japanese into English to read what Yokoi himself had to say about his long ordeal hiding in the jungles of Guam. As near as I could figure, he was filled with fear and shame. At that time, Japanese soldiers believed their emperor was a god. They were taught that if they were captured they would be severely tortured by enemy soldiers, and if they did not die in battle, or commit suicide, they greatly shamed their families.

Yokoi was a survivor, at all costs. So when the US soldiers liberated Guam, he hid in the Talofofo jungle with two other Japanese soldiers, Mikio Shichi and Satoru Nakahata. At first they hid in natural caves in the rolling mountains of Southern Guam. Later, they built separate huts within the jungle. But as Guamanians built new houses closer to the Talofofo River, the two soldiers moved to a cave, and Yokoi dug a tunnel eight feet underground, and ten feet long. In 1964, Shichi and Nakahata died, possibly of poison. Only Yokoi remained as the last straggler, a term Guamanians called soldiers who never surrendered.

On January 24, 1972, Jesus Duenas and Manuel DeGracia found Yokoi while checking shrimp traps in the Talofofo River. Yokoi could still speak Japanese and halting English. He told authorities and reporters how he survived for twenty-eight years in the jungle, the last fifteen years underground.

The only fact that has been disputed is whether Yokoi took part in the murders of two young men in 1950, one the brother of Jesus Duenas. When Yokoi was first questioned, he admitted to being a participant when his comrades murdered Francisco Duenas, 15, and Jesus Pablo, 26. However, later the Japanese government denied Yokoi had anything to do with murdering the two Chamorros.

After Yokoi returned to Japan he was given a hero's welcome, promoted to sergeant, and married. He died September 22, 1997, in Japan at age 82.

Yokoi told his story, and I have passed on this story to you through Kiko's story, which in a way is true, too. It is the story of many secondary rape victims and how, in order to heal, they often go through stages of shock, disbelief, denial, obsession, shame, anger, rage, and retaliation, before reaching acceptance, forgiveness, and healing. However, this is really not a story about war, or hatred, rage, or retaliation. It is a story about forgiveness, redemption, and restoration. For both Yokoi and Kiko.

Acknowledgments

It has been said it takes a village to raise a child. And so, as a book is the child of an author, it is my deep gratitude to these readers who critiqued *No Surrender Soldier* in part or in whole:

Kathleen Ahrens
Jennifer Bradshaw
Pam Calvert
Jody Cosson
Sherry Garland
Michael Green
Kristi Holl
Katy Huth Jones
Julie Knight
Patti Kurtz
Kathleen Muldoon
Christy Ottaviano
Carmen Richardson
Lupe Ruiz-Flores
Anna Webman
Student readers: Robert Jones and Ben Rinehart
SCBWI workshop Arkansas retreat group
Gayle Roper's novel revision workshop group at Mt. Hermon Christian Conference Center

Research Acknowledgments

Pacific Daily News, Gannett Corporation: Publisher Lee Webber and Archive Librarian Carmelita Blas for researching and sending news clips on Shoichi Yokoi.

University of Guam: Richard F. Taitano Micronesian Area Research Center, professor of history and Micronesian studies Dirk Ballendorf, and Archive Librarian Lourdes Nededog for researching and sending news clips on Shoichi Yokoi.

Raymond Baza, musician and composer, of Washington, who answered questions regarding Chamorro music.

Personal Acknowledgments

I'd like to thank my editor Jackie Mitchard for selecting and believing in my story and characters enough to be of Merit for readers. And thanks to Ashley Myers for the final revision notes to refine and polish my novel before publication. Thanks to copyeditor Hillary Thompson; as a former copyeditor myself I know what a tedious job this is, but the polish is in the details.

Last, but foremost, I couldn't have written this story without my traveling companion through life and patron of the arts, my husband, Mike.

Bibliography

28 Years in the Guam Jungle: Sergeant Yokoi Home from World War II, compiled by correspondents of the *Asahi Shimbun*, (Japanese News Service). Tokyo: Japan Publications, Inc., 1972.

Dardick, Geeta. *Home Butchering and Meat Preservation*. Blue Ridge Summit, PA: TAB Books, Inc., 1986.

Farrell, Don A. *The Pictorial History of Guam: Liberation–1944*. *Tamuning, Guam*: Micronesian Productions, 1984.

Gailey, Harry. *The Liberation of Guam: 21 July–10 August 1944*. Novato, CA: Presidio Press, 1988.

Hafa Adai, Guam Visitors Bureau. Tamuning, Guam: The Palms Press, 1988.

Harrison, James Pinckney. *The Endless War: Fifty Years of Struggle in Vietnam*. NY: The Free Press (Macmillan Publishing Company), 1982.

Masashi, Ito. *The Emperor's Last Soldiers*, translated by Roger Clifton. NY: Coward-McCann, Inc., 1967.

Pacific Daily News, Gannett Corporation, various news articles.

Sanchez, Pedro C. *Guahan Guam: The History of Our Island*. Agana, Guam: Sanchez Publishing House, 1987.